FRANCEY

Martin Dubow

Rembrandt Publishing House

ISBN: 978-0-9799771-5-2
Library of Congress Control Number: 2007938103
Rembrandt Publishing House
Tujunga, California
Printed in the United States of America

For my mother—

Who never lost faith

Contents

PROLOGUE

L ORD CRIMSON WAS a self-made man. His vast fortune had been amassed by sweat and hard work, and his title, handed him on a silver platter by the Queen of England. Love, adoration, respect—these he had in abundance. And while a fraction of what he possessed would surely have been enough for any man, for Lord Crimson there was only sorrow and remorse. What horrific crime had he committed that his conscience should weigh so heavily upon him? A good question, but one whose answer had forever remained a mystery, for Lord Crimson had led a good and decent life and had never once failed to let another's needs stand above his own. According to those who knew him best, there was no reason for his sadness. At least, that's how it seemed.

At the outset, let's be clear about one thing. References to Lord Crimson as a young man, and stories of Lord Crimson's rise to fame and fortune, though as interesting and inspirational as any you're likely to hear, will not be found among these pages. The tale with which we are concerned had its start on the day Lord Crimson turned seventy-five and began an adventure that can scarcely be imagined. Perhaps you'd best sit down.

Lord Crimson awoke, on the morning of that fateful birthday, to the usual tugging on his blankets. Without opening his eyes, he reached over the side of his bed to find Charlemagne's neck, and in the hopes of gaining just a few seconds more of precious rest, rubbed it persuasively. The dog, however, would have none of it, and with that annoyingly insistent bark of his, ordered his master out of bed. In grim defeat, Lord Crimson sat up.

"All right boy, you win," he said, and slowly he removed himself from his bed.

Together they walked to the enormous corner window which allowed the morning sun to shine in with a vengeance, and they stood looking out over the vast estate. With a heavy sigh, Lord Crimson bent down and gave his dog a pat.

"I know that technically you're older than I am, but I feel it more than you do, don't I, boy?" The bloodhound whimpered softly and nuzzled his head against Lord Crimson's gentle hand. "Come on, Charlemagne. Let's take a walk, shall we?"

That morning, like every morning, Lord Crimson and Charlemagne made the rounds of the estate. It was just over a mile, start to finish, and while not especially large when measured in terms of the great eighteenth and nineteenth century manors, in modern-day England, it was enormous.

The main house came into view as they walked over the hill toward the end of their hike, and the two friends stopped to rest. His Lordship scanned the countryside, and as his eyes came to rest on the manor, he made his thoughts known to his faithful dog. "Time's run out, Charlemagne. I'm afraid they've given up."

"The post has come, sir," the head butler said, as he opened the door letting Lord Crimson and Charlemagne into the house. "There's a letter from . . . them."

"Thank you, Mr. Portico. I'll be in the living room."

The letter, fetched and brought to his side, Lord Crimson said, "Do me the favor of reading it aloud. I'm afraid I haven't the energy."

"Very good, Milord," the butler said, and with a twenty-four-karat-gold letter opener, sliced the envelope in two. He removed the contents, shook out the single page communication, and holding it at arms length, read as follows:

"To the Honorable Charles Albert Crimson III." Mr. Portico cleared his throat dramatically before continuing.

"Dear Lord Crimson: We regret to inform you that we have exhausted our current supply of ideas and must now insist that you foist your eccentricities off upon one of our other able associates. We will be more than happy to make a recommendation as it would serve no end of delight for us to witness any of our competitors in a turmoil while attempting, futilely, to satisfy your impossible and outlandish demands. We remain very sincerely yours . . . "

Lord Crimson turned to Charlemagne. "I told you, didn't I, boy?" Wearily, he stood up and walked out of the room. Charlemagne tried to follow but was told, firmly, to stay. His Lordship wished to be alone.

For as long as he could remember, Lord Crimson had been plagued with nightmares. Nightmares which remained as much a mystery as the sorrow that seemed interwoven with his soul, for never could he remember even the slightest detail about them. But the cries he heard coming from his lips, and the torment and anguish he felt upon awakening—these he had no trouble at all remembering.

That night, with some trepidation, Lord Crimson lay in his bed. Any added stress always brought with it another unwanted dream, and now, with one more architectural firm giving up the ghost, his distress had become wearisome indeed. The best in London were exhausted. He'd have to look elsewhere. But where?

The dream that night was different in one respect, and even as he sat, bolt upright, screaming, with the tears and perspiration pouring down his face, and his heart attempting to pound its way out of his chest, Lord Crimson realized what it was. Seconds later, when Mr. Portico came rushing into His Lordship's chambers, the butler was greeted by an almost frantic request for pen and paper. The items were quickly rounded up and handed to his Lordship, who then, and hardly knowing what he was about, wrote something down.

"Put this on the desk, please, and we'll decipher its meaning in the morning."

The butler did as requested and then hesitated, his concern weighing heavily. "May I get you something, sir? Perhaps some chamomile?"

Lord Crimson shook his head, but still Mr. Portico didn't budge. He desperately wanted to do something—anything—in order to be of some little use.

"I'm all right, Mr. Portico," Lord Crimson said. "Now please, go back to bed."

The butler bowed. "As you wish, sir. Good night."

The next morning, and for the first time since he'd made

the purchase, Lord Crimson didn't make the rounds of his property. Instead he sat at his desk pondering the meaning of what he had written. Where could the name have come from? How should he act on it, if at all? And then, with a certainty that was as mysterious as the origin of the message itself, he understood that herein lay his final chance. He reached over and gave Charlemagne a pat. "Get Mr. Portico for me, will you boy?" Charlemagne barked and trotted out of the room. A few moments later he returned, with Mr. Portico in tow.

"Milord?"

Lord Crimson handed him the sheet of paper. "Give this to Miss Haversham," he said. "I wish to know if a firm by this name exists, and if it does, I want a meeting with whoever runs the company. Whatever it takes, I want a meeting this week."

Later that day, at the Falstaff Architectural Firm in New York City, the CEO, Johnny Falstaff, and his lead architect, Rick St. Michael, were chatting over a cup of coffee. It was an easy-going, comfortable sort of conversation such as a father and son would have done, had they been close.

"So let me see if I've got this straight," Rick was saying. "This Lord Crimson character is paying you a hundred grand, just for a meeting?"

Johnny shrugged his shoulders and nodded.

"It's a good idea," Rick said. "I mean, at the very least, you could use the diversion, don't you think?"

"I guess. I'll tell you what, though. I'm definitely intrigued. I've done a little digging around and apparently this guy's driven at least a dozen firms stark raving mad."

"What?"

"That's right," Johnny said. "It seems that His Lordship doesn't know what he wants. And at the same time, he knows exactly what he wants."

"I'm not sure I follow."

Johnny chuckled. "Join the club."

The following day found Johnny Falstaff somewhere on the outskirts of London being escorted by Mr. Portico into Lord Crimson's office. Upon Johnny's entrance, His Lordship stood up and extended his hand. Johnny took it and was impressed by the sincerity with which he was greeted. Mr. Portico was dismissed, Johnny was asked to have a seat, the two men looked each other over, and Lord Crimson broke the ice.

"Thank you for making this time available to me."

"It's my pleasure, sir."

Somehow Lord Crimson doubted that.

"Yes, well—before I explain why I requested this meeting, why don't you tell me a little something about this chap who works for you. This . . . Rick St. Michael."

Johnny couldn't help smiling. Rick was probably his favorite topic in the world. Maybe Lord Crimson wasn't as loopy as he'd been led to believe.

"There's an awful lot to tell," Johnny said. "I'm not sure, even, where to begin."

"Why not start with the reason you think so highly of him?" Lord Crimson said. "Tell me why you lit up like a Christmas tree at the mention of his name."

"All right. In a nutshell, the way I feel about Rick is that he's the son I never had. Quite frankly, Rick is without equal on so many levels that—" Johnny caught himself. He loved to brag about Rick's attributes apart from his architectural abilities, but this was hardly the time. Let's focus on the issue at hand, he told himself, and picked up the subject again. "Forgive me—I assume it's his design skills you're most interested in, so let me make it simple for you. Rick St. Michael is the best architect I've ever known. He is, in fact, in a class by himself. Aside from a keen eye and disturbingly good artistic skills, Rick has an uncanny knack for knowing, better than the client, what he wants."

Johnny paused to study Lord Crimson's face. He was touched by the sadness in his eyes and could see that the man needed more. And after a moment's reflection, he went on.

"Something I like even more about Rick, is that even though he's treated pretty much like royalty in most circles, he remains completely unassuming. Not to mention the fact that he could have struck out on his own, years ago. But I gave him his start, and now that our friendship has grown into something we both cherish above almost anything in the world, he remains loyal and will stay at my side forever.

Johnny's expression softened, and his voice took on a whole new aspect. "There *is* one other thing, sir, and to me, it's the most important of all. I've a feeling it will be to you as well."

There was an inherent goodness in Johnny's manner and voice that struck even the granite-laden Lord Crimson, and for the first time in as long as he could remember, his sadness took a back seat to another feeling entirely: Fascination.

"Rick has," Johnny said, "the most unusual—indeed the most extraordinary little girl I've ever encountered. And their love for each other? —It just makes me feel that all's right with the world."

Johnny paused. This was it. "Now, Mr. Crimson, why don't you tell me what it is that I can do for you?"

Two weeks later, Lord Crimson and Charlemagne were standing by the window watching the sunset. Lost in thought, Lord Crimson heard nothing, least of all the butler's entrance to his room.

"Milord?"

Startled, His Lordship turned around.

"Yes, Mr. Portico, what is it?"

"Miss Haversham asked me to let you know, sir. She's just received a phone call from Mr. Falstaff. Mr. St. Michael has agreed to take on your project. He'll be free to start on it next week."

To this, Lord Crimson said, with a desperation lying just beneath the surface, "Let's pray for better luck with this one, shall we, Mr. Portico?" Then, barely audibly, he added, "Because, my friend—I fear the road ends here."

PROLOGUE II

EVERY DAY, AT exactly five o'clock, a school bus
stopped in front of the large, off-white brownstone.
And every day, at that stop, a little girl exited the bus;
for she lived in that brownstone on the very top floor.

"See you tomorrow, Gus," she said, as the bus driver
opened the door for her.

"Count on it," he said, grinning that special grin he
reserved for this child alone.

"Bright and early as usual?" she said, continuing their
everyday banter.

"Bright and early as usual," he replied. And adding to the
daily script, he said, "Now you get inside fast, honeybunch,
'cause it's cold as the dickens out there."

"Come on, Gus, you know the cold doesn't bother me."

"Well, maybe not as a rule, but it's colder'n a dead mack-
erel today, so you'd best not be dawdling."

On this particular day, just as Gus said, it was bitterly, bitterly cold, and immediately after stepping off the bus, a gust
of wind whipped around the corner nearly knocking the little
girl off her feet. The heavy winter coat wrapped tightly around
her might as well have been a silken scarf, given the amount
of protection it afforded her; and the blast of ice-laced air tore
savagely through it, chilling her through to the marrow in her
bones. But instead of hurrying to the steps which lay only a

few feet away, Francey St. Michael stood motionless, absorb-
ing the freezing cold, and allowing it to awaken her soul. And
now, with her awareness heightened to beyond where the
clouds meet the sky, she fixed her gaze on the huge doorway
to her building. There were three flights of stairs to climb,
so she adjusted her backpack for balance and headed for the
entrance.

THE DREAM

THE ST. MICHAEL family consisted of a father and a daughter, and they lived in lower mid-town Manhattan on the east side of the city. Convenient transportation access and the best elementary school on the island were the reasons Rick had chosen that location, and he and Francey were very cozy there.

They were quite well off, Rick being the lead architect at the premier firm in the city—perhaps even the country—and he had purchased the immaculate brownstone a couple of years earlier, renting out the lower three floors and keeping the top floor for himself and his daughter.

The living room had been set up as a studio—a retreat for when he could no longer tolerate the interruptions at the office. Rick's work space was bordered by a wrap-around picture window facing the entrance to the Lincoln Tunnel on one side and the East River on the other. A conference table stretched along the wall to his right and a floor to ceiling bookcase, crammed with a diverse assortment of books, sat against the opposite.

One decoration, alone, adorned the walls. It was a magnificently framed pastel illustration of the *Parthenon* which Rick had drawn filling in the ruined portions so that it appeared, no doubt exactly as it had, when newly built twenty-five hundred years ago. In the last six years he'd had numerous, extremely generous offers to take that piece off his hands, but Francey adored it. In fact, it belonged to her. So it stayed.

Rick had drawn it the year following their first trip to Europe together when Francey had been four years old. Wandering through the ruins in Athens, they had come suddenly upon the aforementioned structure. Francey stood gazing in awe for a few moments before saying "Pop?" She called Rick 'Pop' because that's what he called his father whenever he told her stories of when he was a child. Stories which fascinated her no end as she tried to imagine there were some way possible her father could ever have been a little boy. "Pop," she said, "can we buy that building?"

"Why, sweetheart?" he asked. "Did you want to take it home?"

"No, silly," she said. "You know perfectly well that it would never fit into our apartment."

"Yes, that's true," Rick said, "now that you mention it."

And they went back and forth for a while until Rick had explained to her satisfaction how it wasn't for sale at any price, and it had to remain where it was so that everyone could enjoy its magnificence just as she was doing that day. But they struck a compromise. And thus, the aptly titled *Francey's Parthenon* hung proudly on their living room wall.

Rick sat at his drafting table—in the background, the sounds of rush-hour traffic. He'd been working eighteen hours a day for six weeks or more on a long line of presentations, and now he was designing yet another extraordinary estate in the style of the glorious pre-Victorian mansions for the hoped-for approval from the high and mighty Lord Crimson. And though he'd never met the man, still Rick found himself seeking His Lordship's sanction in a way he'd never sought anything from anyone. As he studied the awe-inspiring design in front of him, this curiosity began to gnaw at him. Who was Lord Crimson that the great Rick St. Michael should care so much? Really. Who?

The sound of a key in the front door broke into his thoughts. As it opened, Rick swiveled around on his stool and watched Francey, just home from school, let herself in. She was all bundled up in her heavy purple overcoat that came down to her ankles, and her purple ear muffs, and purple mittens. But no hat. Because she simply refused to wear one.

"Hey, Pop," she said. "What're you doing here?"

"And I'm glad to see you too," he said, signaling for a hug.

Putting her arms around his neck, she squeezed for all she was worth. "Come on," she said, "you know what I mean."

"There's way too many distractions at the office, and I'm really under the gun on this project. Thus you find me here, hoping for a modicum of peace and quiet."

"I guess I can take a hint," she said. "What do you want for dinner?"

"Doesn't matter. I'm not particularly hungry."

"Well, you've got to eat. I'll let you know when it's ready, okay?"

"Sure, babe. Whatever you say."

"I love you Pop," she said, and gave him a kiss.

"I love you too."

Francey St. Michael was as happy a child as one could ever hope to find. Outgoing, cheerful, caring, she invariably created an immediate bond between herself and anyone who came within her reach. And given her age, she possessed an unnatural maturity. A maturity that many adults never reached. A maturity that put her on an even footing with even the most sophisticated of her father's colleagues. A maturity that enabled her to be, in actuality, Rick's best friend.

While preparing dinner, Francey rehearsed her presentation for the upcoming school day. The story, for the most part, was crystallized in her mind, but she was now deciding to wait until she was in front of the class before coming up with the ending. It wasn't fair that she should know ahead of time how it turned out. It'll just come to me, she told herself. I'm sure it will.

Francey's thoughts shifted to her second favorite person in the world. Sweet, understanding, smart-as-a-whip Miss Gingery. She loved her sixth grade teacher with a passion. When Miss Gingery smiled at her, Francey's life lit up like a thousand suns. And a word of praise from her made Francey feel virtually invincible. What a mom she'll make for some extraordinarily lucky kid, Francey thought, as she methodically went about her kitchen duties. And she imagined herself as that child, for as close and as happy as she and Rick were, still Francey missed having a mother.

The great sadness that would have darkened the little girl's life had been spared her, for she had never known her mother. Sally St. Michael had died giving her daughter life: there were complications, the learned doctors had said, while solemnly shaking their heads. Too many damned complications.

With everything under control and cooking at exactly the right temperature, Francey went into the living room to

watch Rick work. Up until that day she'd never shown particular interest in any of the arts, but even so she was perceptive
enough to see that the design and illustration of pretty much
any type of man-made structure was something her father
could do better than most anyone else alive. Plus there was
the fact that his boss, Johnny Falstaff, who she knew was a
really important man in the architectural world, told her so in
no uncertain terms.

Today, though, as Francey watched Rick while he effort-
lessly sketched a particularly detailed section of the garden,
shading the grass and flowers so perfectly, she found herself
with something to say.

"You know, Pop—"

Rick murmured an acknowledgement, but continued
working.

"You're pretty talented."

Rick put his pen down. It was the first comment she had
ever made regarding his abilities.

"I mean look at this," she said, pointing to the west side of
the house, which he'd drawn with the sun in the background,
just before dusk. "See how the windows reflect the sunlight so
perfectly? And just look at the uniformity and transparency of
the shadows coming off the trees. Do you see it?"

Not sure whether he was supposed to respond to this or
not, Rick's nod was almost imperceptible.

"And here," she said, "the horizon?—see how it drifts off
so perfectly into the sunset? And my God, look at the subtle
blending of the colors in the flower petals. I can practically
smell their fragrance—can't you?"

Francey didn't wait for a reply to this and simply finished
her train of thought. "That's what I mean, you see? That and

a hundred other things I could point out if you asked me to. I seriously doubt if this client of yours needs a work of art this good in order to get the idea. You do it because you're so talented. You have no choice, right?"

Rick took Francey in his arms. High praise had become so integral a part of his life that nowadays he no longer even heard it. But these words from his daughter's lips . . . He held her, waiting for his emotions to settle.

"I think dinner's about ready," she said, struggling to extricate herself from his grasp.

"I'm just going to eat out here, okay? I'm kind of on a roll."

"Okay," she said. "I'll be right back."

Rick was overwhelmed. Not only because of Francey's glowing compliment, but because of the insight she'd shown in explaining her point. Where in God's name did she come up with this stuff?

A minute later, Francey was back, Rick's dinner in hand.

"Thanks, babe. It looks delicious."

"Yeah, right," she said seeing through his faint praise. "You just make sure you eat it."

"I will. Don't you worry."

Francey gave him her sternest look, then turned on her heels and left him alone.

Thinking about what Francey had said, Rick decided he'd wait until later to ask where this sudden interest in his work had come from. Right now, the pressure was building because Lord Crimson was running out of time. A chill ran up his spine and the pen in his tightened grasp snapped in two. What on Earth could have made him think such a thing?

Knowing how important this particular project was, Francey left Rick to his own devices for the remainder of the evening, and with her schoolwork to keep her company, she ate dinner in her bedroom.

Francey was normally meticulous about her homework. Most nights, after the first time through, she'd double check everything to be sure it was one hundred percent correct. That way, she could be certain that Miss Gingery would remain happy with her. Miss Gingery, it can be noted, would have remained happy with Francey no matter what percent correct her homework was, because she loved Francey as much as Francey loved her.

Today, though, the little girl had decided to forego her usual thoroughness. Her teacher, long aware that Francey was bored with the normal sixth-grade reading fare, had slipped her a book on the sly and she was anxious to get started on it.

"Now make sure no one sees you with this," Miss Gingery had said, "because I could get into trouble."

Francey swore to her on an imaginary stack of bibles that no amount of torture could tear their secret from her, and hid it in her backpack.

With her homework done, she took the book from its hiding place. It was titled *Jane Eyre*, and she made careful note of the author's name—Charlotte Brontë. She'd have to ask Pop if he'd ever heard of her. After reading a few pages, Francey discovered, to her delight, that it was about a little girl exactly her own age, and a very grown up little girl she was indeed. Her name was Jane Eyre, and the life that had been thrust upon her was a grim one at best. Francey swept aside her melancholy feeling—there was no way Miss Gingery would have given her something to read that ended sadly—and proceeded to happily devour the pages.

Some hours later, Rick's concentration was broken by the sound of a little girl's voice. "Pop?"

He looked up from his work to see Francey in her pajamas.

"I'm going to bed. You think you can make the time to come say good-night?"

And as Rick stood up, she put her hand into his.

Once in bed, she pulled the covers up to her chin while Rick smoothed her hair and placed a tender kiss on her forehead.

"Listen," he said, "I've been thinking. Once I'm done with this project, I'm going to take some time off and you and I are going to do something—just the two of us."

"Cool," she said, immediately looking forward to whatever it was he might be planning. "So what's this project you're working on, anyway?"

"It's for this British lord. The guy's name is Charles Albert Crimson III, and he's asked me to design a seventeenth-century manor for him."

"Okay. So, what's the problem?"

"Well, let's just say he's a little picky."

Francey gave her father's hand a comforting pat. "You'll get it. You always do."

"Yeah, right. But not if I spend all night in here. So if you don't mind terribly—" Francey's book, lying face down, caught his attention. "What's that you're reading?"

"*Jane Ire.*"

"Oh. You mean *air*," Rick said. "It's spelt kind of funny for how it's pronounced. May I?"

"Don't lose my place, okay?" she said, as she handed him the book.

There were few things in this world that stirred Rick's sadness like Charlotte Brontë's wonderful novel; he ran his fingers over the title page, lost in a memory he no longer shared with anyone else. Francey, of course, would learn of it someday. But for now, this secret would remain between him and Sally.

"Pop?"

Startled, Rick turned to his daughter.

"Is something the matter? You kind of looked like you were taking a trip there for a minute."

"No, babe," he said. "Everything's fine. Now come on. It's time for bed."

Francey pulled him down by the neck to give him a kiss.

"I love you Pop."

"I love you too," he said, and hugged her a little harder, and a little longer, than usual.

Within seconds after he'd let her go, she was asleep. Rick walked quietly to the door and turned around. He mused for a few moments about his precious child and wondered where she could possibly have gotten that book from. He sighed, turned, and got back to work.

Four hours later, he tore himself away from his drafting table and headed for bed.

Rick's bedroom was a monument to the great architecture of the world. The walls were filled with beautifully framed, original paintings of architectural marvels, and the wall-to-wall bookcase overflowed with texts highlighting history's greatest architects. On the ceiling, Rick had painted a replica of a small portion of Michelangelo's handiwork found in the Sistine Chapel. And it would have taken a very discerning eye to tell the difference.

For some time, Rick lay thinking about *Jane Eyre*, and Sally, and Francey, and again he wondered where she could have gotten the book from. The tears stood in his eyes as he thought—as he did so often—of how Francey could have been so much happier, and her life so much more fulfilling, had Sally lived.

Suddenly, from out of the night there came a plaintive cry, and Rick quickly made his way to Francey's room. He peered in, and even in the darkness he could see her tears, for the moonlight shining through the stained-glass window was reflected, jewel-like, from the dampness in her eyes. She called out. And with a voice raised up in despair, and an anguish which grew more painful by the moment, a name fell from her lips. "Edward," she said. "Edward."

With a gentle urgency, Rick shook his daughter. "Wake up, sweetheart. You're just having a dream. Come on now, babe, wake up."

Francey quieted down and a few moments later, opened her eyes.

"Oh, Pop. Hi. Did you just say something?"

"I was just trying to wake you. Get you out of that dream."

"Dream?" she said. "I don't think so. This was too real."

Her comment struck Rick as odd, and he thought about it for a moment before asking if she thought she could get back to sleep.

"Could you stay here with me," she said, "for just a little while?"

"Of course, sweetheart. For as long as you want."

Francey lay silent while Rick took a section of her sheet and dried the tears from her face and the perspiration from her brow.

"Pop?"

Rick gave her a half smile to let her know he was listening.

"I think I know what it's like now to lose someone who's so close to you that it's kind of like both your hearts and souls have gotten all mixed up together."

"Why don't we try and forget about it for now?" Rick said, while, to himself, he damned the nightmare to hell. "If you want, we can talk about it later. Okay?"

"Okay," she said. "Guess I'll see you in the morning then," and she closed her eyes.

It took several minutes for the dream-induced sorrow to completely lose its hold on her, but it did at last. Rick waited at her bedside for a while longer and when satisfied that she was resting peacefully, returned to his bedroom. Sleep, however, did not come so easily to him as it did to his daughter, and he spent the remainder of the night staring at his beautiful ceiling with the same thought turning over and over in his mind: What could she have meant, 'It was too real'? What could she possibly have meant?

THE STORY

RICK WAS ALREADY up. Up, and almost through an entire pot of coffee. It tore Francey's heart out to think that she had contributed mightily to the lack of sleep her father had gotten recently.

"I'm sorry, Pop," she said, putting her arms around his neck.

Rick hadn't even heard her come in. He hugged her back.

"Don't worry about it, okay? I'll try to grab a nap, later."

"You'd better. Promise me."

"I will, sweetheart. I promise."

"How does bacon and eggs sound?" she said, after checking the food supply.

"Great. Just what the doctor ordered."

When the eggs were scrambled exactly the way Rick liked, and the bacon was fried to perfection, Francey served the food, poured two glasses of freshly squeezed orange juice from the beautiful pitcher they'd picked up in Rome the summer before, and sat down to eat.

Rick was lost in thought, and Francey had some thinking of her own to do, so one final time she ran through the story. It's going to be perfect, she thought, and Miss Gingery will be so pleased.

"Hey," Rick said. "What are you smiling about?"

"Well, if you must know, I was just doing some final preparations."

"I see. And what kind of preparations would those be?"

"My teacher—Miss Gingery? She's been working with us on creative writing, and now we're going to try creative speaking. So we're just going to recite. You know—say out loud—stories that we've made up."

"Wow. No kidding? This Miss Gingery of yours sounds pretty cool."

"Cool," Francey said, "would be an understatement of the grossest proportions."

Rick chuckled. "Someday I'll tell you about the old battle axes I had to contend with back when I was in school."

"Oh, Pop, you're just silly," Francey said, in between fork-fuls, as she shoveled the last of her breakfast into her mouth. "Gotta go. The bus'll be here any minute."

She jumped out of her chair and hurried around the table grabbing her books on the way. "I'll see you later," she said, planting a kiss on Rick's cheek. "And tell Johnny, if he gives you any grief about being tired, to call me. I'll straighten him out."

Rick laughed good-naturedly. "Okay, sweetheart. You knock 'em dead."

Rick remained amused thinking about Johnny phoning Francey to get 'straightened out.' The 'Johnny' that Francey was referring to was Johnny Falstaff, president and CEO of the Falstaff Architectural Firm and the only person in the world Rick answered to. He was also one of the most high-powered and influential corporate leaders in America. In architectural circles, Johnny's name was uttered in hushed and revered tones. And when Johnny Falstaff spoke, no breath dared break the stillness. And yet Rick had little doubt that Francey would indeed straighten him out if called upon to do so.

The Falstaff Architectural Firm was housed in a large brownstone on Park Avenue between fifty-fifth and fifty-sixth streets. Rick's office, the coveted one in the corner, was a haven for him. With his door closed, no one would dare disturb him. Excepting, of course, his secretary—the terminally cheerful Beatrice. And though she never took advantage of this privilege, still it occasionally made a retreat to his apartment workspace necessary.

Hoping for a few moments to himself before having to confront Bea's sunny countenance, Rick, quietly, shut his door. But barely had he sat down when his sacrosanct door opened, and with his coffee mug in her hand, Bea made her entrance. She stood for a moment, studying his face. "Jeez, Rick. Rough night?" she said.

"Maybe you'd like to hand me that cup of coffee before attempting to engage me in conversation."

She walked the mug over and placed it in his hand. Silent, unmoving, she watched him take a couple of sips while awaiting an answer to her question. Rick put the cup down. "Francey had this just . . . horrible, gut-wrenching dream last night."

Bea, having raised three kids of her own, felt it hard in the pit of her stomach. "Yeah," she said, "but you know, nightmares are pretty normal for kids. Mine were plagued with them for years."

"I guess," Rick said. "But I swear to God, Bea. Women are so much better suited for this parenting business. I'm not sure how much more of this I'd be able to handle."

Bea's smile had such a comforting way about it.

"You're better under pressure than anyone I've ever seen," she said. "You and Francey—you guys are gonna be just fine."

After she'd left, Rick took a few more pensive sips of coffee. Then, focusing on the plans spread out on his desk, he put down the cup and got to work.

The tiny, well-kept private school made its home in the midst of the teeming city. Surrounded by hovering skyscrapers, waiting for the kill, it fought for its life. Fortunately, it was a historical monument, and a group of conscientious citizens had taken it upon themselves to buck the system and were actually managing to hold at bay the money-hungry wolves salivating to build more, and bigger, profit-yielding buildings for their already very fat coffers. And the Amadeus Elementary School remained standing—an educational oasis amidst a jungle of ignorant, bullying, and arrogant structures.

This was the school that Francey attended. The school in which Miss Gingery taught sixth grade.

In front of the class, a ten-year-old boy, having just finished his recitation, took a bow while the class politely applauded.

"That was excellent, Franklin," the teacher said. "Now, I think we've time for one more."

Miss Gingery smiled at Francey and gave her the nod. As usual, she'd been saving her for last, and Francey bore her lofty station well. Without airs, she walked to the front of the room, and as she looked out over her audience, the story that had been so crystal clear in her mind faded from sight, and in its place stood another. And as it unfolded before her eyes, Francey told the tale.

Gentle reader: there will be no attempt to retell Francey's wondrous story, for she painted a tale of romance, adventure, betrayal, and murder with the grace and style of an

Old Master. And so, in its stead, a sketch is offered sufficient to allow a fertile imagination free rein in which to work its magic.

The setting is a wooded English countryside in the mid-to-late seventeenth century. On horseback, galloping hard, is a young man by the name of Edward Delaney.

In a clearing, deep in the fast-approaching forest, is a magnificent oak tree. On an overgrown root of that massive tree, the staggeringly beautiful Lady Susan Sebastian sits, awaiting her lover. A description of the young noblewoman would put a heavy load upon the quill of a great poet, but Francey finds it child's play, for as she tells the story, it's as if she's there, sharing in the intimacy of that quiet hideout, where Lady Susan and Edward Delaney spend so much time. Planning their lives. Plotting their escape.

As he enters the clearing, and with his horse still at a dead run, Edward dismounts and flies to Susan's side. They embrace. After a moment, Edward tears himself from her arms.

"They are but a few moments behind. I will return for you and we shall disappear forever. My angel, when I think of the happiness that will be ours . . ."

Susan's eyes fill to overflowing as she gazes lovingly at her young hero. Tenderly, yet sternly, she speaks. "Beloved—promise me you will return only if it is safe to do so. If anything should happen to you—"

He places his fingers on her lips. "I promise. And you shall see me again, perhaps sooner than you expect."

One, final, passionate kiss, and Edward mounts his horse.

Barely has he gone from sight when a dozen or more men on horseback, armed with swords and pistols, invade the peaceful setting. The leader, Lord Randolph Trumbull, smirking, the slime oozing from his black soul, approaches Lady Susan.

"Where is he, Milady?"

"Go to the devil," is Susan's cold, calm reply.

"By your father's oath," Lord Trumbull says, "you have been promised to me. And should Edward Delaney meet a tragic end so that I may stake my claim . . . Well, Milady, that will most assuredly be a shame."

Trumbull's smirk turns to a snarl, and kicking his horse bloody, he gallops off, his dozen men close on his heels.

Back in the classroom, Francey was displaying extreme signs of agitation. Her breathing, ragged; her knees, buckling.

"Francey?" Miss Gingery said. "Maybe we should save the rest of the story for another time."

"But I have to finish it now, Miss Gingery. Please let me. *Please.*"

"Of course, sweetheart," her teacher said. "Go ahead."

The little girl turned again to the class, and as if beckoning to them, and just as the children of Hamlin had no choice but to follow the Pied Piper, she led them back to the enchanted land of Edward Delaney and Lady Susan Sebastian.

The setting has changed; it is now early morning in Lady Susan's chambers. Her lady-in-waiting, assisting in the morning rituals, answers the knock at the door. It's Henry, Susan's younger brother.

"Papa requests your presence," Henry says, his voice, trembling.

"May I finish getting dressed?"

"He said immediately."

Hurriedly, Susan makes some last minute adjustments to her accoutrements and follows Henry out the door. Her father, Lord John Sebastian, almost never summons her with such finality and Susan wonders what he could possibly want. She walks into the main chambers to find him, together with Lord Trumbull, seated. Trumbull stands and bows as Susan enters the room. She makes no acknowledgment of his presence.

"You wished to see me, Papa?"

"I am hoping that you will have learned your lesson this time."

Sensing that something is terribly wrong, Susan looks pleadingly at her father.

"Edward Delaney has been caught . . . and dealt with."

She gasps.

"He is outside, if you wish to see him."

Susan rushes to the door and flings it open. The early morning sun, still low in the sky, blinds her as she desperately tries to find Edward. Shading her eyes with her hands, she makes out his figure sitting on a horse. And as her eyes adjust to the light, she sees it all. Edward—tied to the saddle, his shirt soaked with blood, and his head hanging down—is dead.

With a pitiful cry, Susan runs to Edward's side. Her attempts to pull him from the saddle fail, and she falls, choking on her sobs, to the ground. She claws at the dirt, bloodying her fingertips; and over and over again she cries out Edward's name.

Footsteps approach; she raises her head and turns to face Lord Trumbull, who has come outside to catch the show.

"Murderer!" she screams.

And back in Miss Gingery's classroom, a little girl had sunk to her knees; then one last time she wept his name, and quietly passed out.

REMBRANDT

S IXTEEN YEARS EARLIER and fresh out of school, Rick had come knocking on Johnny Falstaff's door. How his portfolio, a few days before, had managed to find its way to Johnny's desk remained a mystery to this day; and now, here he sat, a polite and unassuming young man whose exterior belied the elegance and style exhibited in a devastatingly killer portfolio. Even the preeminent Johnny Falstaff had no choice but to stand up and take notice.

During his senior year at City College, Rick had done an exhaustive study of the best architectural firms in the country. When he had finished, he honed in on Johnny Falstaff and for the remainder of the school year, Rick's focus was on one thing alone: to put together a powerful enough presentation that Mr. Falstaff would have no choice but to take him under his wing.

Rick couldn't wait to get out of school. The rigid, structured curriculum of today's academia offered little of interest to him, and except for the fact that he needed a college degree in order to get a job, he'd happily have left school the day after he'd started. The professors, although competent enough were anything but inspiring, and it appeared that the word *creativity* didn't exist in their collective vocabularies. To Rick's mind, these so-called educators of higher learning couldn't have cultivated a useful architect if their lives had depended on it.

Rick bided his time while studying designs of Johnny Falstaff's own making. After picking two or three choice ones and managing to get hold of the blueprints, he proceeded to make changes: subtle improvements, both structural and esthetic, which he realized would make him seem like a foolish upstart in Mr. Falstaff's eyes, but only for the first few moments. If he could just get by that initial reaction and actually look at what Rick was presenting to him. Tirelessly Rick worked on his presentation, all the while hamstrung by the mundane, lackluster, everyday business of dealing with whatever was thrown at him by his professors. Impatiently he counted down the days until he would, finally, be rid of the educational system's stranglehold.

"So, Mr. St. Michael," Johnny said, studying the young man, carefully, "I understand you're looking for a job."

"Well, sir," Rick replied, "I wouldn't call it that, exactly."

Johnny sat, silent, tapping his finger. His perceptions were keen as an owl's eyesight, but never had he felt as certain about anything as he did at that moment. For the first time in his life, Johnny Falstaff was in the presence of pure greatness.

"What I mean is," Rick said, "I could get just any old job easily enough. I've actually gotten several fairly generous offers since graduating, but I'm not the kind of guy who's going to be satisfied sitting in a roomful of automatons, turning out one more version of some old hackneyed high-rise design. No—it's not a job that I'm looking for—" And quietly, but delivered on a razor-sharp sword, Rick spoke the words that would forever seal their friendship. "What I'm looking for . . . is Johnny Falstaff."

Same setting. Same cast. Sixteen years later. The urgent phone call rapidly wound its way through the Falstaff Architectural Firm, finally ending up in Johnny's office. Johnny picked it up, listened to a few words from the other end, and quickly handed the phone to Rick. An instant later, Johnny was looking at an empty chair. He hit the button on his intercom.

"Bea—a word, please."

Thirty seconds later, Bea walked into Johnny's office. She waited quietly.

"Something's going on with Francey," Johnny said.

"Yeah, I know."

"Then perhaps you'd care to fill me in."

"It's not a lot, but I'll tell you what I can," and Bea sat down.

It was subdued, in the Amadeus Elementary School nurse's office. Francey lay on the bench, her head in her teacher's lap. Enraptured, she listened as Miss Gingery spoke of her father and their trips abroad together—The Louvre; Florence: forever having been his two favorite places in the whole world.

Suddenly, the door flew open, ending—but only for a moment—the gentle quietness. Mute, Rick observed Francey being comforted by a young woman who he assumed was her teacher. No ambulances, no paramedics—just a peaceful scene on a bench in the nurse's office.

"She's okay, Mr. St. Michael. A little frazzled, maybe, but none the worse for wear . . . *Really.*" Miss Gingery smiled, and Rick felt oddly comforted.

Francey, with a little help, sat up. "Hey, Pop, you're here."

Rick picked her up, and with his eyes shut tight, held his daughter desperately in his arms. Miss Gingery found it difficult to swallow; difficult to remember the last time she'd been so moved.

When Rick's panic had finally settled, he and Francey sat down. With his eyes, he asked the teacher what happened.

"Francey was telling a story to the class," Miss Gingery said. "She just got a little carried away, that's all."

Rick needed more, but a gentle hand on his arm stopped him short. "Maybe it'd be a good idea," she whispered, "if we talked about this later." She wrote down her phone number. "Call me tonight. I'll be home around seven."

Miss Gingery watched as Francey and her father, holding hands, walked toward the door. She had to say something—anything—to be of some little use.

"Mr. St. Michael?"

He turned.

"Your daughter is an extraordinary young lady."

Comforted by a voice wrapped in sunshine, Rick tried to thank Francey's teacher for being so perceptive and kind; but alas and alack, the words caught in his throat. Miss Gingery understood, and smiling softly, she nodded.

Francey closed her textbooks. The high priority she normally set for this activity was conspicuously absent, and, though this was a first, it caused her no concern. She simply had things on her mind.

"Pop?"

"Yeah, babe?" he said, putting down his pen.

"Have you ever done any work in oils?"

"Sure, back when I was in school. Why do you ask?"

"Well," she said, "because I was just thinking about Rembrandt, and how great he was. He worked in oils a lot, you know."

Rick simply sat there, fascinated to see where this was going.

"He wasn't only a great artist," she said, as if she were instructing a class in art history, "he was also a wonderful teacher. Warm . . . and patient . . . and so full of love and understanding. A lot of people don't know that."

She smiled, as if remembering a pleasant incident, but said no more about it.

"Do we have any books that talk about the Old Masters?" she asked.

Rick went over to the huge bookcase on the opposite wall and pulled out a large volume. "This book," he said, setting it down on the conference table, "is filled with pictures of some of the greatest works of art ever created. And since you're so interested in Rembrandt, you'll be pleased to know there's a large section devoted to him."

"Thanks, Pop."

She started leafing through the book, and though from where he was sitting he could see only the back of her head, still Rick could feel her intense concentration. Where could this sudden, and apparently consuming, interest in art have come from? And how could she possibly have known what Rembrandt had been like as a teacher? The doorbell interrupted his thoughts. Dinner had arrived.

Francey swallowed what she'd been chewing on and set the double-pepperoni, extra cheese slice of pizza down on her plate.

"Pop?"

"Yeah, babe?"

"You know, it would've been okay with me to fix dinner tonight."

"Yeah, I know," he said, careful to make sure there was no trace of concern in his voice. "I just thought it might do us both some good to relax, okay?"

"Sure . . . Okay."

Francey chewed thoughtfully for another minute or two and then pushed her plate away.

"Pop?"

Rick nodded.

"I didn't make it up."

"Make what up?"

"That story today—the one I told in school."

Rick sighed imperceptibly. Keeping his uneasiness to himself was becoming difficult.

"Are you sure you want to talk about this?" he asked.

"Sure," she said. "Why not?"

Rick pushed from his mind the dozen or so reasons he could have given her and said, "Okay. I'm listening."

"Well," she said, "there I was in front of the class, and the story I was all set to tell suddenly disappeared and another one—the saddest story you could ever imagine just popped into my mind. But I wasn't making it up. I was remembering it—just like I remember stuff from yesterday."

"An actual memory?" Rick questioned. And though what she was saying had to be fantasy, not a hint of disbelief was in his voice.

"Yeah," she said. "And it probably wouldn't have been quite so sad for me, except that I was remembering it through Susan's eyes."

"Who's Susan?"

"Lady Susan Sebastian. My tragically beautiful seven-teenth-century heroine."

Rick nodded for her to go on.

"Anyway, when I . . . she . . . saw Edward—"

"Edward?"

"Edward Delaney—Susan's lover." The melancholy smile that had been on her lips turned to a quiet sadness, and she faltered for a moment before continuing. "So when I saw him tied to that saddle, with his shirt all wet with blood . . . Well, I guess you can imagine. And you want to know what his crime was? It was that he loved Susan. And she loved him too. She loved him so much that it hurt. Anyway, I'm okay now. I still remember the whole thing, but I'm okay."

Francey used her napkin to blot away her tears. "Do you mind, Pop? I'm not really that hungry, so I think I'll just get started on my homework."

"Okay, sweetheart. I'll see you later."

Rick's mind was numb with overload. Last night's dream. Today's Rembrandt discussion. And now, this supposed memory. Then he remembered the phone call, and he wondered that he felt so relieved at the thought of talking to Francey's teacher.

ALEX

THE DISTANCE FROM the Amadeus Elementary School to Miss Gingery's apartment was seventeen blocks, and come rain, snow, sleet, or hail, she always walked it. The route she took lay close to the East River, and the wind whipping off the water added to the already frigid wind chill factor bringing it to zero degrees exactly. Freezing cold, and with her eyes locked onto only what lay straight ahead, Francey's teacher had two things on her mind. And like a razor sharpened by the bone-chilling cold, her mind honed in on them.

In general, men held very little interest for Miss Gingery, if for no other reason than she could never seem to find one who came anywhere close to measuring up to the two in her life who had long since laid claim to her affections: her father, and her little brother.

Struggling to keep from smiling for fear the icy cold would crack the skin around her lips, Miss Gingery thought about that afternoon, sitting close to Mr. St. Michael—Christ, she didn't even know his first name—she'd have to check the student records—and watching him with Francey. How he adored her, protected her, would have sacrificed anything for her. And then, when though it had been only for a moment that their eyes had met, her instant perception of an innate wit and wisdom, with more than a dash of sensitivity and compassion thrown in, made her quite aware that her heart was still alive and kicking. God help her if Alex should find out about this. His big sister actually showing an interest in some guy? He'd have an absolute field day.

The lonely whistle of a barge floating on the East River broke into her thoughts. She glanced around, taking stock of her surroundings. Just a few more blocks. Thank God.

But shelter from the freezing cold played only a small part in Miss Gingery's determination to reach the warmth of her apartment. She was seeking an answer. An answer which she hoped would be found among her father's books, for Francey's tale today had been no mere story conjured up by a child's imagination. It had been a richly detailed, moving narrative of incredible depth, as lifelike as anything she'd ever experienced. And reliving the tragedy, real tears began to intermingle with those that had already been wrought by the Arctic-like wind.

She turned the corner and her stride lengthened to its limit. Much like the champion long distance runner inching ahead of the field just before the finish line, every last ounce of the sixth-grade teacher's energy was concentrated on the entranceway to her building.

Upon hearing the door open, Alex, lying on the sofa, placed a bookmark in Charles Dickens' enormous novel, *Bleak House*, and sat up.

"Hey," was his usual greeting.

"Hey, yourself."

"Oh jeez, Lizzie," he said, checking his watch, "I'm sorry. I meant to have something ready for dinner, but if you think about it, you've only got yourself to blame."

Alex and his cryptic remarks. Lizzie waited to hear the explanation for this one.

"You're the one who told me I should read this book, re-member? So I picked it up and, well . . ." He shrugged his shoulders apologetically.

"Not that I accept the blame for your blatant irresponsi-bility," she said, teasingly, "but don't worry about it. I've got some research to do and I can't be bothered with anything as trivial as eating, right at the moment."

"So you don't mind if I just keep reading?"

"Do whatever you like. Not that you wouldn't anyway."

Her smile was amazing, and the way her eyes sparkled. Alex thought it was one of the neatest things about his big sister, never suspecting that he, too, possessed that same, dazzling, disarming smile.

Alex had arrived in town only a few days earlier. Though just having turned sixteen, he had already graduated from high school and was trying to figure out what to do with the rest of his life. An intense dislike for school ruled out so-called higher education, and since he had an enormous amount of respect for his sister, Alex was hoping that if he were to spend some time with her, his future would, with her guidance, sort itself out.

One particularly interesting thing about Alex was that although he was a healthy, heterosexual teen-aged boy, he gave every appearance of having very little interest in the fairer sex. And because he possessed those dashing good looks one usually associates with swashbuckling pirate tales, filled with sword fights and romantic trysts; in addition to a radiant smile that had been able to melt the hearts of even the coldest, and most dispassionate of his female teachers, it was to the great dismay of the girls at his school that, no matter the tactics they employed, their feminine wiles were pitifully useless when directed toward gaining Alex's favor.

There was much conjecture as to why this was so, but Alex wasn't concerned. To him it was a matter of honor. Somewhere, there was someone waiting for him. Who she was, or how he knew this, mattered little. And armed with this knowledge, he had no choice but to remain faithful.

After preparing a pot of coffee, Lizzie took it, along with an enormous mug, and shut herself up in her bedroom. She surveyed the wall-to-wall bookcase she'd had specially built in order to make room for her warehouse-sized collection of books and selected several large one-of-a-kind volumes circa the time-period, and location, in question. She set them on her desk and before setting about her task, took a long, deep draught of coffee.

Jonathan Gingery had been a man of many and diverse interests. His greatest passion of all, though, had been the study of genealogy. Countless hours had been spent poring over old family trees, centuries-old portraits, and ancient life histories. Without so much as a passing thought, he would travel half way around the world upon discovering that one more volume containing the long-lost facts of some well-known, or even not-so-well-known family from a bygone era had turned up for sale. And no matter the cost, if it were a legitimate find, he would make the purchase and blithely add it to his already incomparable collection. He had left all of his books and notes to Lizzie, whose interest in the subject, up until that day, had been mild at best. But in the time it had taken for Francey to tell her story, her interest had turned all consuming.

Lizzie removed the oldest, largest, and rarest book from the stack and stared at the cover. What in the name of all that was holy did she think she was doing? Did she honestly believe that somewhere between the covers of one of her father's books she would find Francey's storybook characters? It was sheer lunacy, but still she turned back the cover and began her search. Painstakingly, and page after page, she studied each entry noting dates, names, places. Her patience quickly grown thin, she picked up the pace. Faster and faster she scanned the pages, until with the rapidity of machine-gun fire, she tore through the book. Then, suddenly, she froze; the sound of her heartbeat exploding in her ears. In disbelief, Lizzie touched the page, running tremulous fingers over the portrait. As if awaiting judgment for unspeakable crimes against his daughter, Lord John Sebastian stood before her. Amidst an array of emotions too numerous to chart, a chill ran up Lizzie's spine. Fleetingly, she thought about what it could mean, but she thrust it aside; she'd wonder about it later.

Her doubts had been shattered; now she was a huntress, seeking her next prey. At last she had him in her cross-hairs, and she sickened at the sight. Lord Randolph Trumbull, in all his arrogance, stood smirking at her from three and a half centuries past. The slime oozed from the page, and she wiped her hand to rid herself of it, for her fingers had accidentally touched his picture. A sensation she'd never before felt hit her hard—Vengeance.

The contents of that book exhausted, she opened the next, and with her observational skills now working at full tilt, it didn't take her long to find the next cast member. When she had, she paused to spend a moment with a sweet, innocent, good-looking boy, while trying to imagine what it could have been like for Henry Sebastian to have been besieged by such tragedy.

Then, knowing somehow what would immediately follow the picture of Lord Sebastian's youngest child, Lizzie, her heart beating hard enough to drive nails, shut her eyes and turned the page. Cautiously, she peeked underneath her eyelids and in the tiniest fraction of an instant, her world was shaken, then shattered, and finally pulverized, leaving Lizzie standing, knee-deep, in the dust of all that had been, but was no more. Lady Susan Sebastian was exactly as Francey had described her—from the color of her eyes, to the playful tugging at the corners of her mouth, almost, but not quite, turning her portrait-proper expression into a smile. My God, she was beautiful. Beyond beautiful. She was breathtaking. The vitriol Lizzie had felt at her encounter with Lord Trumbull dissolved as if to nothing, while the love rising from Francey's fairy tale heroine took her to her bosom. But even with the evidence literally staring her in the face, and though she had dared to suspect she would find exactly what was in front of her, still Lizzie doubted her senses.

She scoured the rest of the books looking for some mention of Edward Delaney. But there was none, and she realized why. Portraits, with their prohibitive costs, were reserved strictly for the upper classes. Susan Sebastian's young lover, alas, didn't qualify.

Lizzie sat slumped in her chair. How could Francey have known about these people? And even more baffling, how was it possible that her knowledge could so far surpass what had been set down in recorded history? Lizzie reached for the phone and realized she didn't have the number. Well, if she couldn't get it through information, she'd go back to the school and rifle the student records. If necessary, she'd break in. And just as her hand touched it, the phone rang.

A moment, please, to shed a bit more light on Lizzie's lack of enthusiasm regarding the male species of the human race.

Nine years earlier, Lizzie had accompanied her father on a trip to Naples to inspect a manuscript that had surfaced during an excavation near Mt. Vesuvius. The document turned out to be quite a treasure, and though he had to pay a small fortune for it, Jonathan was ecstatic. To celebrate, he decided they should extend their stay an extra week, and they hopped on the next train to Florence.

Lizzie fell hopelessly in love with the enchanted city and for the first few days, wandering the streets with Jonathan, lived as if in a fairy tale. Then the beautiful and innocent nineteen-year-old college girl met a man. Perhaps if she hadn't already fallen victim to the spell of the ancient city her feet would have remained firmly on the ground. But the allure of Florence, combined with an irresistible Italian accent, made the temptation difficult to resist, and without a struggle, she succumbed.

Jonathan, of course, held no illusions about the typical Italian male, and though he knew his words would fall on deaf ears, made a half-hearted attempt to warn his daughter that the slick-sounding sincerity which dripped from the lips of her new friend bore no resemblance to the truth. Lizzie wouldn't be convinced and Jonathan, reluctantly, but wisely, let the ill-fated romance run its course.

On their final night in Italy, while Jonathan was in the hotel room, packing, Lizzie burst in, threw herself on the bed, and buried her head in the pillows. Jonathan, wordlessly, sat down beside her.

After a few moments, Lizzie unburied her head.

"Well, why don't you say it?"

"Say what?" he asked.

"I told you so. I deserve it, don't I?"

She waited for a reply and when none came, searched her father's eyes—those deep, steely-gray eyes which had never once wavered from being in her corner. Had she been standing, her pang of conscience would have knocked her to the ground: in her entire life, Jonathan had never made a single judgment about any of her foolish decisions.

"Oh Dad, I'm sorry," she cried, and threw her arms around him.

"There, there, my darling," he said. "There, there," and after a few moments, he unwound himself from her grasp. "I want to show you something."

From his wallet, fetched from atop the bureau, he took a photograph and handed it to his daughter. It was of a little girl—four years old, perhaps. To Lizzie's perceptive eye, there were several remarkable things about her; chief among them: she was a child whose thoughts would never dwell ill upon anyone, and who carried in her pocket enough comfort and compassion to leave a liberal trail of it, wheresoever she might choose to go. Lizzie marveled at the sight; the child's soul was the most beautiful thing she'd ever seen.

"Who is this?" she asked.

"You don't know?"

Lizzie shook her head.

"It's you, sweetheart."

Numb, and disbelievingly, she stared at the photograph.

"I don't show that to many people," Jonathan said. "Maybe a handful since it was taken. And those select few who've seen it, have all, each in his own way, said the same thing. Would you like to hear?"

Her eyes overflowed. And she raised them to hear her father's words.

"It is not possible that the little girl in the photograph is born of this Earth. But since she has somehow found her way here, let us be thankful, for the planet cannot help but be a better place having received a visit from her."

Jonathan took Lizzie in his arms, and holding her with the love that only a father for his cherished daughter possesses, said, "Somewhere out there is a man, who, when he looks into your eyes, will see you just as you did when first you looked upon the little girl. And when your paths finally cross, if you're yet unsure, then ask yourself this: What would Dad think? Would he like him? Would he trust him? And most especially, would he approve of him courting his precious Lizzie?"

With a wistful smile, Lizzie picked up the phone. There was no doubt whatsoever how Jonathan would have felt about the father of the incredible little girl.

"Hello?"

"Miss Gingery, it's Francey's dad."

"Oh, hi. I'm so glad you called."

Already comforted by the sound of her voice, he said, "I just wanted to let you know that Francey gave me quite a descriptive account of what happened today."

"No kidding? I'm kind of surprised she was willing to talk about it."

"She was more than willing. She insisted."

"Well . . . that's good I think. But if you don't mind," Lizzie said, "I'd like to tell you what happened, from my point of view."

"Of course," Rick said. "Go ahead. Please."

"I believe," Lizzie said, "that today I was closer to a miracle than I've ever been in my life. Your child told a tale that swept away not only her classmates, but also her somewhat cynical and often jaded teacher. We were—all of us—transported, body and soul, to another time, where the characters she painted were so lifelike that even now I feel as if I could simply reach out and touch them. And in the end, as the tragedy descended on the class?— Oh my God."

Lizzie waited a moment, letting her emotions settle. "My tears drenched Francey's face as I carried her to the nurse's office, and later, when I'd finally gotten back to my class, I was greeted by a group of little statues. No evidence of so much as a blink or a whisper. It was an effect the likes of which I've never even imagined—

"Wait," she said, sensing that Rick was about to say something, "there's more." And Lizzie prepared herself for the task of tearing asunder the mind and soul of another human being.

"The picture she painted was so detailed . . . so incredibly realistic, that I couldn't just leave it alone, so I've been doing some research."

"Research?" Rick said. "What do you mean?"

"Well, I'll tell you. I have this huge collection of genealogy books, and I've been looking up the names of the people in the story. Crazy, huh? But I had this feeling." She took a deep breath. "They're all there. Every last one of them. Just exactly the way Francey described them."

"What? But that's impossible."

"I agree. Nevertheless . . ."

"Actually," Rick said, "suspending reality for a minute—in the context of what Francey told me tonight, it makes sense. But it's still pretty much the most unbelievable thing I've ever heard."

What?" Lizzie said. "What makes sense?"

"Francey told me she has actual memories of those people—that she remembers them just like she remembers stuff from yesterday."

"Oh my God," she said, and was now left struggling against a silence that Rick finally ended.

"I guess I should get going," he said. "But . . . Well . . . I just wish I could express how much I appreciate all the trouble you've gone to."

Lizzie assured him that it was no trouble, and told him that if he or Francey needed anything more from her, to simply ask. Neither of them wanted to hang up. Her voice was so comforting to him, and his was reassuring to her that here, at last, was a man worth the trouble. But impossible to answer questions brought with them a turmoil making conversation difficult. And, alas, they had no choice but to say good-bye.

"It's open," Lizzie said, to the knocking on her door. Alex peered in, and at the uncommon sight of sadness in his big sister's eyes, he walked over to her bed and sat down.

"You want to talk?" he said.

Lizzie shook her head no.

"Come on. Since when do you have qualms about confiding in me?"

"I don't have qualms," she said. "It's just that I'm not at liberty to discuss it. So please don't ask. Okay?"

Alex nodded. "Okay, so what do you want to do?"

"Sweetheart—I'm still in the middle. I'm sorry."

"Well then, I guess I'll just have to be satisfied spending the rest of the evening in the company of Sir Leicester and Lady Dedlock," he said, referring to two characters from *Bleak House*.

"Has Inspector Bucket come on the scene yet?" Lizzie asked, attempting to display at least *some* interest in Alex's activities.

"Not yet. Why?"

"Well, because he just might be my favorite character in all of literature."

"Wow, no kidding? Then I look forward to meeting him," Alex said, as he swung Lizzie's bedroom door shut behind him.

THE MISSING ELEMENT

RICK GLANCED OVER at the clock sitting at the edge of his drafting table. Past Francey's bedtime, he went to check on her. Settled in at her desk, she was well into *Jane Eyre.*

"Hey, kiddo," he said. "Bedtime."

"One sec," she said, as she finished off the paragraph. She put a bookmark in place and with great care closed the novel. Then she slid it to the upper right hand corner of the desk, lining it up perfectly with the edge, and got into bed.

"Pop?"

"Yeah, babe?" he said, as he sat down by her side.

"I was thinking, before, about this afternoon, when I was with Miss Gingery in the nurse's office."

"Yeah?"

"Yeah. She was telling me about her father. She really loved him a lot, you know, and they did all kinds of things together. Just like you and me."

"Loved? Past tense?"

"Yeah, he died. I guess a couple of years ago."

"That must've been pretty rough for her."

"It was . . . but you know what she says?"

"No, babe, what?"

"She says that his love of life was so infectious, and that her memories of him are so vivid and wonderful, that when she thinks about him and all the incredible things they used to do together, that it's almost like he's still here. Right by her side."

"Sounds to me like you and Miss Gingery are awfully good friends. I mean, pretty much only best friends are comfortable talking about such intimate things."

"Really, Pop? Really and truly?"

"Yeah, really and truly."

Rick's words filled Francey with pride.

"You know what I told her?" she said.

"Nope."

"I told her that that you and I had exactly that kind of relationship. *Exactly* that kind. And you know what she said?"

Rick shook his head.

"She said I was a lucky child. I mean, that's all she said, but there were tears in her eyes when she said it, and then she hugged me. And then we both cried a little bit. I guess that's kind of an unusual thing for a kid and her teacher to be doing, huh?"

"It *is* unusual. It's so unusual that I don't think I've ever heard of anything quite like it before in my whole life."

"Wow," Francey said. "Wow."

Alex lay asleep on the sofa with *Bleak House* lying open on his chest. Lizzie gently lifted the book and placed a bookmark in it. She sat down and touched her brother's shoulder.

"Hi."

"Hi," Alex said, rubbing the sleep out of his eyes.

"I have a question for you."

"You *do* realize that I was fast asleep."

"Yeah, I know. I need to ask you something."

"Okay, I'm listening."

"Good. Now here's the question. Did you ever find yourself in a quandary? And I don't mean over some silly little problem. I'm talking about something on the scale of the meaning of life, or whether or not the universe has any boundaries."

"Maybe not quite that monumental," Alex said, after a moment's thought, "but I've found myself embroiled in some pretty heavy stuff."

"Okay. Good. Now I'm not asking for the sordid details, I just want to know what you did about it: how you came up with the solution."

"Simple," Alex said. "I asked Dad to help me."

"Dad's dead."

"Yeah, no kidding. But he wasn't when I needed him. And it's really not necessary to remind me that he's dead."

"I'm sorry. It's just that . . . Well, since you mention Dad—I sure could use his help, right about now."

"Lizzie, listen to me. Except for our father, you're the smartest person I've ever known. Whatever's going on, if there's an answer, you'll find it."

"Yeah, right," she said, "there's only one problem."

"And that is—?"

"Whatever the answer is, the thought of actually finding it scares the hell out of me."

The following morning, Rick was back at his Park Avenue desk. A backlog of paperwork due to too many days away from the office was threatening to take his entire workspace hostage. At the light tapping on his door, Rick looked up. Strange. No one but Bea would dare interrupt him when the door was shut, and she never felt it necessary to knock. "It's open," he called out, and Johnny Falstaff walked in.

A few words should suit us, right about now, regarding the Falstaff Architectural Firm's illustrious leader.

Though himself an extremely competent architect, Johnny Falstaff had other capabilities. Capabilities that placed him stratospherically above the level of ordinary men. A case in point—merely one anecdote drawn from hundreds—will help shed some necessary light.

While in his senior year at Brandeis University, Johnny had been called upon by his classmates to run for student president. Due to his low opinion of politicians in general, the thought of taking part in any sort of political arena made Johnny's skin crawl, and he resisted it as best he could. But the relentlessness of his fellow students paid off, finally convincing him that the changes which so badly needed to be made could actually be brought about if the right person were in office. Johnny, reluctantly, threw his hat in the ring.

His opponent was a young woman named Kate Raleigh. She was bright, articulate, good-looking, and popular as all hell. No one but Johnny would have stood a chance. The night before the election, a rally was held at Johnny's campaign headquarters, and just for the hell of it, Kate Raleigh sneaked in to listen to Johnny's rousing last minute speech. The result was something that to this day is still talked about by the alumni. That night, after the rally, Kate withdrew from the race. And one month after graduation, Johnny Falstaff and Kate Raleigh were married.

These were the charismatic leadership qualities that Johnny Falstaff brought with him into the architectural world. And along with another of his extraordinary gifts—that of being an enlightened teacher—he found himself to be a magnet for the most talented architects around, enabling him to assemble a firm filled with the best and the brightest in the field. Under his wing, these young men and women were patiently guided until heights, formerly only dreamed of, were attained and surpassed. The Falstaff Architectural Firm was now, and had been for some years, almost without exception, the first choice for any great, unique, or extravagant project, and it was not even arguable that Johnny Falstaff was the most influential man in his field.

"You busy?" Johnny asked.

Rick simply looked at him, knowing it couldn't be good news. He nodded for Johnny to make himself comfortable. Johnny sat down and handed Rick an e-mail. Another rejection from Lord Crimson.

"Listen, Rick," Johnny said, intending to suggest that maybe he should take a break from the Crimson project. What with all the other turmoil Johnny could sense was going on in his life, the added stress of trying to satisfy the fanciful whims of a man whose sanity quite a few people were now seriously beginning to question probably wasn't helping matters.

"Yeah, I'm listening," Rick said.

There was an uncommon coolness in Rick's tone, and Johnny decided it was probably best to leave it alone. "Never mind," he said. "Never mind."

Johnny, once back in his office, opened up the portfolio

containing Rick's rejected submissions—each more astonishing than the last. What in holy hell could Lord Crimson
be thinking? He shut the portfolio and walked over to his
window. Gazing down at the Park Avenue traffic, his thoughts
reached back to the one other time he had felt such deep concern for his friend.

Rick had been with Johnny for a few years and their
friendship had grown strong. It hadn't taken long for their
wives to become drawn into their little circle, and Sally and
Kate had quickly become best friends. What a conniving pair
those two had been. Johnny smiled, in a grave sort of way, at
the memory of Kate and Sally plotting scheme after scheme in
their attempts to broaden their husbands' cultural horizons;
the results of which were Rick and Johnny finding themselves
at ballet recitals and symphony concerts a bit more often than
they'd have cared for. But they all loved each other with a passion, and the men took it all in stride.

During Sally's pregnancy, she and Kate were inseparable.
Shopping; planning; decorating—this was a newborn child
who would want for nothing. Kate helped Sally with it all and
was always close by. Right up until the end.

Johnny's throat tightened, recalling how Rick had carried
on after finding out it was going to be a girl. The things they'd
do; the places they'd go; and oh my God—the dollhouse he was
going to build for her. The plans had been drawn up, and the
materials necessary to create a dollhouse the likes of which no
little girl had ever set eyes upon had been ordered. And then,
with a flick of fate's finger, it had all come crashing down.

It was Kate who brought the little girl home from the hos-
pital, and it was Kate who cared for the child, while Rick lay in

his bedroom, alone with his grief. And for as long as she was needed, Johnny's wife lived at Rick's apartment, seeing to the infant's needs and doing what she could to be of some little comfort to the child's father.

Johnny rarely dwelt upon those black times, but today it loomed strong, casting a shadow on his every thought.

Rick sat at his desk staring at the rejection letter. Before Lord Crimson's appearance, criticisms of any kind were few and far between. And flat-out rejection? Non-existent. The fact that so many people around him had quickly become convinced that Lord Crimson's eccentricities bordered on downright lunacy made no difference. Because lately, he'd begun to suspect that something was missing. Something so close and intimate that he could almost taste it, and yet its elusiveness caused it to slip from his grasp every time he closed his fist around it. This puzzle, stacked on top of the mysterious goings-on surrounding Francey, for anyone else, would have meant certain and utter defeat. For Rick there could never be such an option. He would die before surrendering.

He filled his portfolio with his current sketches; and back-logged paperwork be damned, he headed for the exit. On his way, he peered into Bea's office.

"I'm going home."

She nodded. "I'll make sure you're not disturbed."

"Good. Thanks."

"Any idea when you'll be back?"

And because this conversation had already taken far too long, Rick said, "I'll be back when I'm done, okay?"

"Sure Rick. See ya." Bea's eyes trailed sadly after him as he walked, hurriedly, toward the exit. It was the first time in all

the years they'd been together that he'd been even the slightest bit short with her.

The sixth-grade class was unusually well-behaved that
day. Not that they weren't, ordinarily, but today there was
something curiously subdued about them.

Lizzie studied her children and soon realized that they
hadn't recovered from the story-telling incident. Every child
in her class—first one, and then the next—glanced fleetingly
at Francey, and then, hoping she hadn't noticed, went quietly
back to his or her work. Courage was being gathered, and finally one little boy raised his hand.

"Yes, Danny?" Lizzie said.

"Miss Gingery? I was wondering . . ." Danny hesitated,
and the class, still as marble figurines, waited for his question. "Could Francey tell her story again?"

Lizzie scanned the children's faces. She'd never seen such
eagerness. But it was out of the question. "I'm sorry, Danny. I
really don't think that's a good idea."

"I don't mind," Francey said. "I could tell a different part.
A happy part. What about if I did that?"

"Are you sure, sweetheart?"

"Absolutely."

"Well, then . . . Okay."

She stood now in front of a group of children, so anxious
they could scarcely catch their breath; and quickly found,
while searching through her past of long ago, the perfect
thing. And so began the tale anew.

"In a clearing, deep in the forest, there stands a giant oak
tree. Its overgrown roots, so comfortable to sit upon, are large
as pythons, recently fed; and its spreading branches are so

thick with leaves that though the sun were born again a dozen times moreover, within the shade cast by that mighty tree, midnight's silent blackness still would hold you in its clutches. It is here, within this secret and secluded spot, that two forbidden lovers meet in clandestine rendezvous—safe from small minds and prying eyes—to speak of love and plan their future. A future, as we learned so recently, which would prove to be fatally thwarted by the powerful Lord John Sebastian, and the mean and dastardly Lord Randolph Trumbull."

Francey smiled through the outbreak of boos and hisses; today she would speak only of joy and happiness.

"What was Edward like, Francey?" called out one little girl who had stood up to better make herself heard. "Tell us again. Please?"

"Okay, Patty," Francey said. "Even at the risk of embarrassing him, still, I will."

Francey waited patiently as Patty sat back down, rested her chin in the palms of her hands, and with unblinking eyes, handed Francey all the attention she had in this world.

"If you can," Francey said, "listen in your mind to laughter that sets butterflies to light upon your heart while returning the gaze of a boy whose eyes grant you entry to a soul so full of love and life and happiness, that you want to take it in your hands and set it free to roam the lands, and seas, and mountaintops; its wondrousness enabled then to change the world, forevermore. Add to that a smile, which, when shone upon you removes the strength from all your limbs, leaving only his embrace to keep you from sinking, like a rag doll, limply to your knees. Imagine these which I have just now set before you and you shall have but the barest beginnings of an answer to the question, 'What was Edward like?'"

Dreamily, all the girls sighed.

"What about Lady Susan?" called out one of the boys.

"Lady Susan," Francey murmured. "I'll tell you in Edward's words, because I don't think I can improve on them."

But the child faltered and her eyes threatened to fill as a long-forgotten love scene faded into view. She spent a moment waiting for her composure to return.

"Yes," she said, "I see them now secure within the oak's low-hanging boughs. Wrapped in each other's arms he kisses her . . ." Whereupon an overwhelming rush of passion and sorrow swept through the little girl, staggering her.

"Sweetheart?" Lizzie said.

"It's okay. I'm okay . . . But is there some way I could sit down?"

Lizzie quickly carried her chair over and stood close by as Francey seated herself.

"Thanks."

Lizzie nodded, and after returning to her desk, cleared off a spot and made herself comfortable.

"Okay," Francey said, "so they've just kissed, right? And it was such an amazing, amazing kiss. Now his arms are tightly wrapped around her waist, but it's as if they are also wrapped around mine. His eyes embrace me with a love I cannot begin to describe, and an angel's voice sweeps me off to an uncharted Neverland. Hush, children, and listen—his soft words, like a garland of roses picked just before dusk fall gently 'round my head.

"'Beloved,' he whispers in my ear, 'if there be not a Heaven, then one must be created, for the most beautiful creature ever to tread upon the Earth must have a proper home in which to spend eternity.'"

A BROKEN CUP

MUSING OVER RICK'S most recently rejected submission, Lord Crimson sat at his desk. Mr. Portico entered. And standing quietly by, he awaited the reason for his having been summoned.

"We'll be making a short trip to the States tomorrow," Lord Crimson said. "Please ask Miss Haversham to make the necessary arrangements."

"Very good, Milord."

As Mr. Portico turned to carry out his orders, Rick's illustration caught his eye.

"Is that the Falstaff Firm's latest offering, sir?"

Lord Crimson nodded, and Mr. Portico walked over to have a look. In one instant, the butler's opinion of Americans was shattered beyond recognition.

"It's quite extraordinary, sir, don't you think?"

"Yes," Lord Crimson said, "it *is* extraordinary."

"What I mean to say, sir, is that it's on an entirely different plane of existence from anything any of our boys have thrown together for you, isn't it?"

"Yes, it is."

"But still no?"

Lord Crimson shook his head. He picked up the drawing and after spending a few moments in reflection, raised his sad eyes to Mr. Portico's.

"Entirely aside from the unearthliness of its beauty, there is something which raises this man's work, further still, above the others. It's something which gives me, perhaps for the first time, an iota of hope."

That he was one of but a select few with whom Lord Crimson spoke of intimacies gave Mr. Portico a feeling of self-worth such as nothing else could. And fairly bursting with pride, he waited to hear His Lordship's innermost thoughts regarding the remarkable architect.

"He has come to understand," Lord Crimson said, "that something is missing, and the search which has been mine alone for so many years has become his as well. This is a relentless man—I see it; I feel it; and what I'm hoping—indeed what I'm praying for—is that he has better luck in finding it than I have done."

"Is he the reason we're going west, sir?"

"No. He's made no effort to make my acquaintance. I'm afraid our business on this trip is other than with the Falstaff Firm."

"And if he *had* expressed a desire to meet you?"

"Then I would make myself immediately available to him. Our business interests aside, this is a man whose friendship, I have little doubt, I should find worthwhile."

"I daresay," the butler replied, and he went in search of Miss Haversham.

The front door opened.

"You're home early," Rick said, looking up from his work.

"Early? Jeez, Pop, it's after five."

He looked at his watch and sighed. "Hey look," he said. "Don't worry about dinner, okay? We'll just order out."

Francey finished hanging up her stuff and walked over to give Rick a hug and a kiss.

"You know what?" she said. "I think it's time you stopped treating me like an invalid. I'll handle dinner and you needn't worry your pretty little head about it."

"You sure?"

"*Pop.*"

"Okay, okay, whatever you say."

As Francey turned to go into the kitchen, she noticed that on the conference table were several volumes opened to illustrations of huge mansions of a bygone era. She walked from one to the next, studying each one briefly.

"Are you building one of these?"

"Yeah. That is, if I can ever get Lord Crimson to approve the design. I still haven't quite been able to nail it down."

Francey inspected the pictures more closely while Rick went back to his work.

"Pop?"

"Yeah?"

She walked over to him and put her arm through his.

"I'll help you . . . if you want me to."

"What do you mean? Help me with what?"

"With what you're doing, silly."

Rick put his pen down.

"I'll tell you what'll help me. You go fix yourself some dinner, then do your homework, and call me when you're ready for bed."

"Okay," she said, as she headed for the kitchen. "Let me know if you change your mind."

Rick, warmed by Francey's good intentions, wondered for a moment what she would have done if he'd taken her up

on her offer of help. Then, focusing on what lay in front of
him, he bulldozed everything else out of his mind.

Rick came up for air. It was considerably past Francey's
bedtime and since dinner he hadn't heard a peep out of her.
He found her, curled up in bed, fast asleep, with *Jane Eyre*
lying open next to her. He bookmarked it and placed it on her
desk, lining it up exactly with the edge, just as Francey did
so lovingly every night. Then, before getting back to work, he
smoothed out her covers.

One hour later, while taking a break and halfway through
a cup of coffee, the calm, quiet of the night came to an abrupt
and savage end. The cup at Rick's mouth dropped, crashing to
the table, as the sounds of terror all but shattered the walls of
the apartment. This was no pastoral scene, reminiscent of the
other night, that greeted Rick as he burst into his daughter's
room. She lay writhing on the floor, her fingernails digging
into the rock-hard oak panels. Through wracking sobs, Rick
heard the now familiar name cried out; and with his entrance
to her room Francey raised her head and turned to him. "Murderer," she screamed.

Quickly Rick knelt down. "Francey, wake up," he commanded. But she didn't wake; and with blazing hatred in her
eyes, she once again screamed—"Murderer!"

Rick's attempts to bring her to her senses grew increas-
ingly more forceful. And though his voice remained steady, its
laser-like intention was enough to slice a diamond down the
middle.

At last he'd gotten through, and as the dream cut loose its
stranglehold, Rick's sigh of relief ended the most frightening
moments of his life.

"Oh, Pop," she cried, holding onto him for dear life, "he's dead. Murdered. And it was my fault. All my fault." Francey took a few deep and ragged breaths, gulped down one last sob, and took back control of her life. "Hey," she said, "how come you're still dressed?"

"I'm working. But let's not worry about me right now. We need to get you back to sleep."

"No thanks. At least, not in my current frame of mind. Maybe I could come keep you company for a while?"

Rick reached out to take her by the hand.

On the way to the living room, Francey glanced into the kitchen and saw, on the table, a once-treasured mug, now irreparable.

"Oh no, Pop, it's your favorite cup." She went to the table and lovingly picked up some of the broken pieces.

"It's only a cup," he said. "We'll get another one."

"Not like this. Don't you remember? In Florence?"

"I *do* remember, and I admit, I was very fond of that cup, but it's still only a cup. If we can't find one like that, we'll find another one, just as nice. Okay?"

Sniffling, Francey dried her tears with her pajama sleeve and slipped her hand into her father's.

"Promise?"

"I promise."

Rick sat down at his drafting table; Francey pulled a chair up beside him. With the added stress of this latest nightmare, he was exhausted beyond his limits and without thinking, he folded his arms on the table and lay his head down.

"Pop?" the little girl said, her hand upon his shoulder.

He grunted some kind of an acknowledgement.

"Maybe you should get some sleep. The work'll still be here in the morning."

"Yeah, I know. It's just that I'm on a roll here, and I want to work on it while it's still fresh in my mind."

"Well, what about just taking a nap? I'll be okay here. I just wanted for us to be in the same room . . . Please?"

"I guess a short nap can't do any harm." Rick stood up and tested his legs to make sure they'd hold his weight. Then he fetched his alarm clock, set it to go off in half an hour, and sank into his recliner. He watched his daughter as she sat at the conference table, poring over the illustrated pages of ancient homes. But before he could let her know that he was only going to grab a half hour's sleep, he was already gone.

THE MIRACLE

T HAT SOMETHING IN particular happened to trigger the miracle is not up for debate. What it was, however, will no doubt be discussed for some years to come. Be that as it may and whatever it was—that night, it grabbed ahold of the little girl and forever after held her in its grasp.

Francey took a box of pastels from the middle drawer of Rick's drafting table and from the cabinet above, she removed a large sketch pad. Uh oh, the alarm clock, she realized, and without a second thought, shut it off. She made herself comfortable, and with the sure hand of an artist, began to draw. Questioning how this could be happening didn't occur to her because it felt as natural as writing an essay about how she'd spent last summer; and without so much as glancing up from the task she'd set out for herself, worked until dawn. Her labors now completed, and the light of day just beginning to glimpse over the horizon, Francey folded her arms on the table, put her head down, and went to sleep.

Rick opened his eyes to the sounds of rush hour traffic and the warmth of sunlight flooding the apartment. Damned alarm, he thought, and then noticed Francey asleep at his desk.

"Francey, wake up," he said, his hand on her shoulder. "The alarm didn't go off."

In a fog, she opened her eyes.

"I can't understand it," Rick said. "I know I set it."

"I turned it off."

Rick was stunned. He realized she'd done it for him—so that he could get some sleep—but it was so unlike her to do something this irresponsible.

"Pop, I'm sorry. You were so, so tired, I just had to let you sleep. And I knew I could finish your picture for you."

Rick turned to where she was pointing, and there lay what the miracle had wrought. Several illustrations, each from a different angle, of a mansion. Detailed, lifelike, exquisitely rendered; drawings he'd have been proud to call his own. And a thunderbolt hit him square on the side of his head. This was the house Lord Crimson was looking for.

"See?" Francey said. "I told you I could help you."

Numb, Rick nodded.

"It's Papa's estate," she said. "I was just a little girl when it got built, so I guess you could say the house and I grew up together."

"What about this one?" Rick said, pointing to a view drawn from above looking down on the rooftop. "How could you see from this angle?"

"There was this enormous oak tree on a hill. And every day I'd climb way up to the tippy top 'cause it was just so peaceful up there, and I would sit for hours just admiring the house and the countryside."

"Sweetheart," Rick said, "who did you mean before, when you said Papa . . . Papa's estate?"

"Papa . . . My father . . . You know—Lord John Sebastian."

Rick peered into Bea's office. "Hi."

"Hi," she said. "You're back."

"Yeah. Any chance I can get a cup of coffee?"

"Coming up."

Their late start had precluded Rick's having a wake-up cup at home and withdrawal was setting in. Finally Bea walked into Rick's office and handed him his mug.

"Sorry," she said. "If I'd known you were coming in, I'd have had a pot prepared."

Bea watched as Rick took those first welcome sips.

"Is Johnny in yet?" Rick said.

"Yeah, but I need to warn you. He's pretty worried."

"Well, hopefully I can put his concerns to rest."

"I wish you would. He's been bugging the bejesus out of me. You know—'What's happening with Rick? Have you heard anything from Rick?'"

"Hey, that's pretty good," Rick said, referring to her excellent Johnny Falstaff impression. "You should do that for Johnny sometime."

"Yeah, right," she said, chuckling, and turned to leave.

"Bea?" Rick said.

"Yeah?"

"Listen. About yesterday? I'm sorry. Really, really sorry."

She smiled, letting him know he'd already been forgiven.

"You're back."

"Bea's exact words," Rick said, as he put his folder on Johnny's desk. Normally, Johnny would have come up with a rejoinder, but today he simply accepted Rick's offering and pulled out the contents.

"I'm going to need a day or so to turn it into a proper presentation," Rick said, but Johnny was already lost in the artwork. Carefully he studied them, one after the next; and when done, he went through them again.

"There's something about these," Johnny said. "I can't explain it, but somehow they just feel right. You know what I mean?"

Then, as carefully as if he were handling priceless manuscripts, Johnny returned everything to the folder.

"I'll set up a meeting with Lord Crimson," Johnny said. "As it turns out, he's here for a couple of days, so it looks like you're finally going to meet the man himself."

"All right," Rick said. "Just let me know where and what time."

Rick had just reached the door when Johnny spoke again; this time with quiet words as cold as ice: "If he doesn't like this, I'm telling him to take his business elsewhere."

"He'll like it," Rick said. "This is the house that he's been searching for."

LIZZIE'S PLACE

L IZZIE, WITH HER back against the headboard and surrounded by volumes large and small, sat on her bed. Having twice painstakingly combed through one of the most comprehensive collections of genealogy texts on the planet, she almost certainly knew more than anyone else alive about those tragic souls—which, sadly, wasn't terribly much, for their role in history wasn't vital. Desperate to know more, there remained only one other place to look, and she reached for the phone.

"Hello?" Rick said.

"Mr. St. Michael, it's Miss Gingery."

"Miss Gingery . . . Hi."

"I was wondering," she said, "I've pretty much exhausted my research materials and—well, I think if I could just talk to Francey. That is . . . If it's all right with you."

The thought of Miss Gingery's company was anything but unpleasant and if the circumstances had been any other—but alas, they were what they were.

"Here's the thing," Rick said, with a reluctance that wasn't lost on the sixth-grade teacher, "Francey had another nightmare last night, so I'm trying to keep things limited to activities not embracing the realm of the supernatural."

"A nightmare?" Lizzie said.

Strange, he thought, that he'd spoken as if she'd already been aware of them. And stranger still, as he hadn't felt comfortable discussing the subject with anyone, period, Rick was at ease, and even relieved, as he related, in painfully graphic detail, the terror of the nightmares.

"How awful. How awfully awful," Lizzie said. "The poor child."

It's no wonder Francey adores her, Rick thought, listening to the compassion in her voice.

Lizzie, however, wasn't about to give up and waited for something to come to her. It took all but an instant. "How about this?" she said. "What if *we* meet—I mean, just you and me? If nothing else, you've got to be dying for somebody you can talk to."

"No argument there."

"Well then, do you know the Starbucks near the school?"

Rick was amused. He knew where every Starbucks in the city was, and the one by Francey's school was an especial favorite of his. From the picture window in the coffee shop was a clear view of the Amadeus Elementary school, brazenly sitting there amongst the huge skyscrapers and the noisy hustle and bustle of the churning city. The sight of the little red schoolhouse fighting for its survival and actually winning always made his coffee taste better.

"Intimately," he said, "but I don't have anyone I can leave Francey with."

"Bring her over to my place. My little brother just got into town, and he's great with kids."

"Uh . . . How old is this little brother of yours?"

"Sixteen."

The idea of leaving Francey with some teen-aged boy he'd never met didn't meet with Rick's instant approval. Lizzie was amused; equating Alex with the normal teen-aged boy was fairly preposterous.

"Let me set your mind at ease," she said. "Alex is the most responsible kid this planet has ever seen. Infinitely more so than most adults I know. And should it come down to it, he'd protect Francey with his life."

"Sounds like quite a boy."

"I love him to death."

He took a breath. "What's your address?"

Rick peered into Francey's room where she was hard at work on some homework or other. He watched her for a few moments, admiring her intense concentration as she sat at her stunning walnut desk; aside from *Francey's Parthenon*, her favorite possession in the world.

The original had been on display in the window of a little antique store in Paris, just off the *Champs-Elysées*. Francey had spotted it from across the street and had dragged Rick into the shop insisting that it was exactly the right size, shape, and color she needed in order to give her homework its proper due; and had demonstrated that fact by sitting down at the desk, a make-believe pencil in hand, while doing some pretend-homework. Sadly, it was outrageously overpriced, so it remained where it was. But Rick, on the sly, took a picture of it and shortly after they'd returned home, he drew it out, specs and all and had his favorite artisan turn it into a magnificent piece of furniture—nicer by far than the original, due to various esthetic changes he'd made in the process. The look on Francey's face when he'd surprised her with it on her birthday would forever remain as one of his fondest memories.

"Hi Pop, what's up?"

"Get your coat, sweetie. We're going out."

"Out? On a school night?"

"Yep."

"But my homework—"

"Don't worry about it. Miss Gingery'll understand."

Francey's radar immediately went up. Why in the world would Miss Gingery understand? "And might I be so bold," she said, with her hands firmly on her hips, "as to inquire just where exactly we're going?"

"You'll see."

"*Pop.*"

"Just humor me, okay? I guarantee you're not going to be disappointed."

"Well . . . Okay."

Lizzie took a moment to regroup. Alex wasn't going to be overjoyed at the news that she'd committed him to an evening of babysitting, especially in light of the fact that she'd been ignoring him for the past couple of days. Well, she thought, as she put the books back in the bookshelf—he'll thank me in the end.

Alex was stretched out on the sofa, almost half-way through *Bleak House*. Lizzie envied her little brother the rapidity with which he was able to plow through a book. And if that weren't enough, he retained every little detail of everything he'd ever read. It was mind-boggling.

She pushed his legs over to make room for herself and sat down. "You'll be pleased to know," she said, "that I've taken the liberty of arranging a very pleasant evening for you."

This ought to be interesting, Alex thought.

"You know this research I've been doing?" she said.

Alex rolled his eyes to assure her that he hadn't forgotten the reason she'd been ignoring him.

"Well," she said, "there's this young lady in my class—Francey—"

"Francey? No kidding?" Alex said. "Shades of *A Tree Grows In Brooklyn*—no pun intended."

"Very funny," Lizzie said, "and it's not spelled the same. Now . . . may I continue?"

Alex folded his arms in an intent listening posture and nodded.

"Thank you," she said. "Anyway, regarding this research, there's something I need to discuss with her dad—"

"And, pray tell, what's *his* name?"

"Actually, I don't know his first name, and it's not really important because we have a parent/teacher relationship, so I call him Mr. St. Michael and he calls me Miss Gingery. Now, may I tell you this without further interruption? Please?"

Alex gave her a well-behaved nod.

"As I was trying to say," she continued, "there are a few things that he and I need to discuss and since he doesn't have anyone he can leave his daughter with, I thought it might be nice for you—and for her too—if he brought her over here. That way, even though you'll be without my scintillating company for the evening—"

Alex quickly put the pieces together. Here was Lizzie, consumed by something so sensitive that she wouldn't divulge it even to him—the one person to whom she'd always felt free to communicate pretty much anything—and it was definitely looking like this little kid, Francey, was at the heart of the matter. This appeared to have the makings of a fairly interesting evening.

"You can spare me the sales pitch," Alex said. "I'm happy to do it."

"Thanks, sweetie, you're a doll," Lizzie said. "And I think I should warn you—this is a child the likes of which you've never before encountered."

Alex chuckled to himself. He was already aware of that fact.

Ten minutes later, Rick and Francey were standing outside Lizzie's door. Rick's evasiveness regarding their destination finally got the best of his daughter. "Pop," she said. "I demand to know whose apartment this is."

Now that they'd arrived and there'd be no time to answer awkward questions, Rick, as he knocked on the door, revealed their whereabouts. But Francey didn't question it because she was too busy coming to grips with the idea that Miss Gingery actually had a life of her own outside the classroom. Of course teachers must have had lives—she'd just never thought about it before. And now, faced with this revelation, Francey waited eagerly as the sound of footsteps from the other side of the door grew louder.

As Lizzie passed the sofa, Alex looked up from his reading. "Hey," he said. "Did you just put on makeup?"

Lizzie disdainfully ignored the question and opened the door. "Come on in, you two. It's nice and toasty in here," she said, for a light layer of snowdust lay on their heavy coats.

Francey loved the snow, at least when it first started to fall and the dirt and grime of the city hadn't had a chance to, as she loved to say, 'slush it all up.' And no matter how cold and hard the wind blew, she never felt it, for she imagined the snow as one huge, billowy down blanket, its warmth wrapped tightly around her.

As if in a dream, Francey stood in Lizzie's living room. That she could have been a part of her teacher's life, outside of the classroom, had never entered the sphere of possibility; and the surroundings grew even more surrealistic as she watched the boy lazily remove himself from the sofa and walk toward them. She admired the easy way he carried himself and the self-assured manner in which he shook hands with her father. Then her heart paused, just for an instant—he had turned toward her.

"And Francey," she heard Miss Gingery, a faint voice from afar, say, "I'd like you to meet my little brother, Alex."

Her little brother, who was at least half a head taller than Miss Gingery, smiled his most disarming smile, and said, "Charmed, Milady." He took her hand in the gentlest way she could ever have imagined and kissed it. And there she was, back in the land of enchantment. Noble heroes, beautiful damsels in distress. Dragons. Witches. Who could this wondrous boy be that he conjured up these images? She knew him somehow. From a far-off somewhere. A far-off long ago . . .

"The pleasure is mine, good sir," she said. And in keeping with the kiss on the hand she'd just received, she curtseyed. Vaguely, Francey heard Alex say to Miss Gingery and Pop, "You guys take off. And don't worry about us, okay? We'll be fine."

A few moments later, after having barely been aware of Rick hugging her, along with some hazy 'good-byes' and 'see you laters,' Francey found herself alone with Alex, sitting at the kitchen table. She listened, spellbound, for he was about to say something.

"So, Milady, what's your pleasure? Croquet? Cricket? Darts? Or perhaps a spot of tea?"

She studied the boy's face, making note of his devilish good-looks and bright and sensitive face, and she wondered at how comfortable she felt in his presence. Then a smile came over her, and she paid him the supreme compliment. "You're silly, Alex. Just like Pop."

The room seemed to glow with the radiance of his smile. Where on Earth had she seen it before? Obviously it was just like Miss Gingery's, but that wasn't it, and there was no time to think about it now because he was waiting to hear what her pleasure was.

"What I'd really like to do," Francey said, "is draw your portrait. Would that be all right?"

"Me? Really? Sure, if you want."

Alex saw to her drawing needs and returned to his chair.

"Turn your head just slightly to the right," she said. And to the trained eye, the illustrations she had done for Rick's project would have appeared as simply a warm-up exercise, for what appeared on that blank sheet of paper which sat upon Lizzie Gingery's kitchen table, though done only in pencil, was a work of art such as hadn't been created on this planet in the past several hundred years.

COFFEE

ESPECIALLY AT NIGHT, the quiet snow always brought with it a calming influence to the city; even the cab drivers were not so quick to lean on their horns. The swirling whiteness wrapped itself around the street lamps, softening the glare; and Rick and Lizzie, comfortable in each other's company, walked silently along; snug within the fantasy of Francey's huge down blanket.

"It's amazing, don't you think?" Rick said, after they'd both taken seats and had their first sips of coffee.

"What's that?"

"The school. The little red schoolhouse standing bravely among the mighty skyscrapers. I can almost hear it challenging them: 'I'm here to stay, so back off before I get rough.'"

Lizzie looked out the window. She must have had a thousand cappuccinos in this place and yet it had never occurred to her before. What kind of man is it who perceives something like this? Lizzie gazed at the endearing scene and imagined the Amadeus Elementary School throwing down the gauntlet. She loved the school, and she adored teaching there. But especially, she loved the little girl in her class who had made it possible for her to meet a man who possessed qualities for which she'd long ago given up the search.

"So, is that something for me to look at?" Rick said, his attention on the folder lying on the table.

Nodding, she slid it over to him.

"Before I look at this," Rick said, "I'd like to ask you kind of a personal question."

"Okay," she said. "Shoot."

"This is a little awkward, since I feel like we've already been through the wars together, but . . . What's your first name?"

The sound of Lizzie's laughter was a quiet musical composition, played by the string section of an orchestra. Mozart, Haydn perhaps. Rick looked at her a little more closely, and the weight on his shoulders shifted, lightening the load just a bit.

"It's Lizzie."

He reached over to shake her hand.

"Hi, Lizzie. I'm Rick St. Michael."

"Hi, Rick."

"Thank the Lord that's over with," he said, returning her smile, and Lizzie struggled to keep from touching him. Even in the midst of this incredible upheaval, still he was able to make her laugh. Leave it to Francey to have a father like this.

Rick ran his fingers lightly over the folder. Where its contents would lead lay beyond his wildest imaginings, and slowly, cautiously, he turned back the cover.

"That's Lord Sebastian," Lizzie said, as Rick studied the first portrait. He nodded, but didn't look up; and turned to the next.

"The gruesome Lord Randolph Trumbull," she said, and though it was subtle, she perceived his revulsion at the sight.

"Henry," she said, when he'd turned the page. "Susan Sebastian's younger brother."

She held her breath as he turned to the last. And as Rick stared at the young, tragic noblewoman, Lizzie tried to imagine what he was thinking; feeling. She recalled how—in the nurse's office—she'd wanted to take his hand. To be of some comfort. And now, at that moment she might have, had Rick not closed the folder and put his hands in his lap.

"There's no picture of Edward Delaney," he said. His voice, quiet; masking a turbulence that trembled the floor beneath them.

"No, there wouldn't be," she said, "because he was a commoner. His family couldn't have afforded such a luxury."

"I see. You said before that you wanted to talk to Francey. Can I ask . . . what about?"

"I wanted to show her these portraits—to see if she recognized them. And maybe ask her some questions, depending."

"Listen, Lizzie," Rick said. "Something else happened that I haven't dared mention a word of to anyone. It's at least as unbelievable as this is. Maybe more."

Lizzie nodded, her smile, faint but reassuring. She was willing to accept, entirely without judgement or evaluation, whatever it was he was going to say. It had been a long time since Rick had felt so safe.

"After the second nightmare," he said, "as you can imagine, Francey didn't want to be left alone, so she came into the living room—that's where my drafting stuff is set up—to keep me company while I worked on this fairly pressing project. But first she begged me to take a nap because . . . Well, I'll tell you about it some other time. Anyway, I conceded, and while I was asleep, she shut off the alarm and spent the rest of the night working on my project."

"I'm not sure I understand," Lizzie said. "I mean, you're an architect, right?"

"Hang on, it gets better. First, what you need to know is, I'm not just an architect. I'm actually a fairly well-respected guy in the architectural community—"

As understated as this comment was, still it caused him enormous discomfort; it was the first time in Rick's life that he had blown his own horn, but he needed to communicate the magnitude of what Francey had done. Lizzie'd forgive him.

"—but I was at a loss with this one. Every one of my submissions has been summarily rejected, with no explanations. So there I was, plagued by this for the past two months, and this morning I woke up to find that, not only had Francey finished my project, but—and don't ask me how I know this—the house she designed is the one that will end my client's lifelong search. And to really put this into perspective for you, they weren't just drawings. They were absolutely stunning works of art."

Lizzie listened, absorbed in astonishment, as Rick told her of the conversation he'd had with Francey afterwards. How the house she'd drawn had originally been built in the seventeenth century. How she'd watched its construction from the top of the oak tree. How she had called Lord Sebastian, 'Papa.'

Done with the telling, Rick grew still as death. There existed no words of comfort for his distress; though Lizzie might well have tried, had the wind not been so completely knocked out of her by a fantastic thought. And Rick waited for his turn to be astonished as Lizzie's rosy-hued complexion turn white as Francey's unslushed snow.

"Just give me a sec," she said, while catching her breath. "It's something I just remembered . . . about Susan Sebastian. And I know it's crazy for me to think that this has any actual relevancy, but . . . Susan Sebastian was a brilliant artist. More than brilliant. She, apparently, rivaled the great masters of her time."

Francey had long since stopped using Alex as a reference point for her drawing. Every detail in his face had become fused with her soul and taking even brief moments to glance at him would have interfered with her concentration.

Out of curiosity, and every once in a while, Alex shot a glimpse in her direction, and finally realizing that she was no longer using him as a guide, he turned in his chair and made himself comfortable. A concentration like nothing he'd ever seen shone through those hauntingly beautiful green eyes, while the pencil, held in her perfect fingers, moved with such an easy confidence that he found it almost disturbing. So wonderful was the sight of this child that Alex would have been content to sit there forever, watching her draw.

At last she set the pencil down on the table and looked up.

"May I see?" Alex asked.

She nodded and handed him the drawing. It was of Alex, on horseback, decked out in seventeenth-century garb. Older—perhaps in his early twenties—but unmistakably it was Alex astride that horse. The subject matter, however, was secondary—even superfluous.

Both Alex and Lizzie, under their father's tutelage, had studied extensively of the Old Masters. In addition to what they'd learned at Jonathan's side, a considerable amount of time in all manner of art museums had been spent. Their studies had, in fact, taken them to many far-off lands, and so it was with a practiced and expert eye that Alex viewed the portrait in his hands. This drawing done off-the-cuff by the little girl across the table could have hung, no questions asked, in any museum in the world: in the Rembrandt wing, was his educated guess. He tore his eyes from the artwork and fixed them on hers. Who, in God's name, was this child?

"That's you in seven years," Francey said.

Blankly, Alex nodded.

"Don't you like it?" she asked.

Doesn't he like it? Alex struggled to say something. "It's—" he steadied his voice. "How did you do this? How could you possibly have drawn this?"

Francey just smiled. She loved creating this effect. First Pop, now Alex. "Uh oh," she said, looking at her watch. "I completely lost track of the time. Pop had wanted me in bed half an hour ago."

Mr. St. Michael didn't seem like the kind of guy whose wishes should be trifled with, so Alex put his ten thousand questions on hold.

"Lizzie put clean sheets on her bed for you," he said. "Come on, I'll show you her room."

Francey lay in Lizzie's bed, thinking. Not about the miracle that had been sent her in the form of artistic abilities far surpassing those of living mortal men, but of Miss Gingery's magical little brother. She knew now why he'd seemed so familiar when first she'd set her eyes on him. Though, for the time being, she thought it best to keep it to herself.

Alex, at the kitchen table, studied Francey's drawing. The shading and detail, the subtle expressiveness in the eyes, the perfectly rendered folds in the clothing; but most unsettling of all was her flawless use of light and shadow—a technique utilized by Rembrandt on a level that no one before or since had any hope of approaching. Alex, one of the planet's more grounded-in-reality people, was doubting his senses. What he'd witnessed was simply not possible.

Then from Lizzie's room came a cry; and something stirred inside him. He rushed to the bedroom and when he saw, bathed in moonlight, the anguish upon the little girl's face, Alex's blood ran cold. He'd been here before.

Again, and yet again, she cried out, "Edward . . . Edward." Quickly, Alex went to her; and merely at his approach, her tortured cries melted away. Then, with a tenderness that made his heart ache, she said, "Oh Edward, you're alive. I thought—oh, my darling, I thought . . ." She then reached out and took his hands in hers, and after kissing them, turned over, fast asleep.

Alex was in the kitchen working on a freshly brewed pot of coffee. Upon hearing activity at the front door, he turned the drawing face down on the table.

The snow was coming down hard now, and the bitter cold showed on their faces. Lizzie's hair, wet with snowflakes, glistened almost as brightly as her eyes. Alex's big sister always looked so alive, but with her hair and her eyes sparkling like this, it was a spectacle.

"Well," she said, "everything seems peaceful enough. So—no broken bones?"

"No," Alex said, staring at the overturned drawing. "No broken bones." He looked up at his sister. "She's really something, isn't she?"

Lizzie smiled in response.

"So," Rick said, "what did you guys do, anyway?"

Alex put his hand on the sheet of paper. To assure himself that it actually did exist. And without a word, he turned it over.

Too late to stifle the gasp, Lizzie's hand flew to her mouth. And numb, Rick collapsed in the nearest chair; his thoughts, dizzied—a cyclone, out of control.

It was a silence wrought of turmoil that permeated Lizzie's kitchen, and as quietly, as gently as she knew how, Lizzie sought to break it. "This is you, sweetheart . . . Right?"

"Yeah. Francey said that's me in seven years."

Silence again. But Alex had another incident to relate. He wished it could wait—at least long enough to give them a chance to absorb what they'd just seen. But they needed to know.

"Guys," he said, "there *is* one other thing . . ."

Then, and with no less attention than they'd have given the Second Coming, Rick and Lizzie listened to the story of the 'bedroom incident.' The dream, the anguished cries, the name she so agonizingly called out; and finally, the sudden and happy ending. Valiantly, Alex struggled to get through it without succumbing to emotions remindful of what he'd felt at his father's funeral. And managed, until the last few words.

"She kissed my hands," he said, "and then she drifted off, just peaceful as can be. It was the most touching thing—"

But unable to continue, Alex stood up and turned his back

only to then feel powerful arms folding around him; and with muted tears, he returned Rick's embrace.

Lizzie was almost as astonished by this as anything else that had happened in the past few days. Alex hadn't shed a tear since shortly after their father's death. He had sworn to her, two months after Jonathan died, that he'd never cry again. 'There'll never be anything of a magnitude worthy of tears,' he'd said, 'now that I've had to deal with Dad's death.' An unbroken vow, up until only a few moments before.

"It's late," Rick said. "I should take Francey home."

"I'll get her for you," Lizzie said. And she went to gather the child.

Sweetheart?" Lizzie said.

Rick and Francey had been gone for several minutes, and Alex was staring into his cup, yet to utter a word. He nodded, letting her know she had his attention.

"Do you remember the first time Dad took us to the Louvre?"

"I was barely out of my infancy," Alex said, "but I do have some recollection of it."

"God he loved that museum, didn't he?"

"Yeah. He'd've moved in if they'd let him."

Lizzie picked up Francey's drawing. She held it delicately; as if it were a bubble about to burst.

"How is it possible?" she said. "I mean, how is it even possible?"

He attempted no answer.

"Oh God, Alex," Lizzie said, "if only Dad were still alive."

Then, for a little while, they reminisced about their father and of the extraordinary places he'd taken them. And their talking jogged Lizzie's memory. "Let me ask you something," she said. "When's the last time you visited the Met?"

"You mean the museum?"

"Well I don't mean the opera."

"Hey, I've been to the opera. In fact, I like it. You shouldn't be so dismissive."

"Sorry. You're right. So . . . When?"

"I don't know. It's been a while I guess. Why?"

"All right. Here it is," Lizzie said, getting down to business. "I've had a field trip there planned for over a month, and my assistant came down with something. So what I need is a replacement for her or I'm going to have to cancel. You want the job?"

Alex loved the Met. Short of the Louvre, it was his favorite museum in the world. But he wouldn't give in without at least a slight struggle. "What is it," he said, "like fifteen or twenty screaming brats?"

"It's eighteen, to be exact, and they don't scream, and for the most part, they're not brats. So?—Yes or no?"

Alex, mockingly, heaved a sigh. "How can I possibly refuse those irresistible charms of yours?"

Lizzie laughed. "Well, with that last piece of business settled, what do you say we get some sleep?"

"You go. I'm gonna need to chill for a bit."

"Not too long, okay? You're going to need your strength to keep all those little hellions in line."

The smile in her voice was plain, but Alex heard nothing: he was a million miles away.

Alone now, Alex feverishly tried to fit the pieces together. He pictured Francey in her despair, and with a resounding *crack*, the connection between them tightened like a massive padlock on the gates of hell. A gate which—though their bodies were as if bound together—still separated them inexorably; and the fiery bowels dragging the little girl toward its blazing core brought a cold sweat to his brow: if the key unlocking that gate weren't found soon, the child was doomed.

THE INCIDENT AT THE MET

ALONE ON FRANCEY'S desk, *Jane Eyre* lay. Neglected for an entire day, she missed the company of the little girl whose fingers caressed her pages, and whose razor-sharp mind invented insightful solutions to the many plights in which the young heroine found herself. It was so comforting being held in her hands. Perhaps tomorrow.

Rick, with Francey asleep in his arms, sat on the edge of her bed. She clung to him, her arms around his neck. Several times he attempted to set her down, but each time her grasp grew tighter. So he held her, and humming a song that Sally had loved, was reminded of a similar incident; though it was so long ago.

Rick lay in bed, staring at the ceiling. There was a soft tapping at the door before it opened, and Kate peered in.

"Ricky," she said. Of all his friends, Johnny Falstaff's wife was the only one who called him by his youthful nickname. "Ricky—your daughter's asking for you."

Blankly, he stared at her. Francey was just barely a day or two old. How could she be asking for him?

"She wants her dad," Kate said. "She needs him to hold her. To assure her that she's not to blame."

Even through his grief, a pang of conscience all but crushed his broken heart. Of course she wasn't to blame. He must see to it immediately—fix it, if such a thing were possible with a child newly set upon the Earth.

On trembling legs, weak from disuse, Rick followed Kate to where Francey lay awaiting her brand new father's arrival. At his appearance her eyes shone bright and a smile seemed to flicker across her lips. And then, as startling as anything he'd ever heard, or even dreamt about, the infant raised her arms and reached out to him. Rick, in disbelief, turned to Kate to verify what he was seeing. Above her soft weeps and flooding tears, Kate smiled and nodded.

Gingerly, Rick picked up his daughter. Her arms, still outstretched, reached around his neck and as she clung to him, he clung to her as well—their love for each other filling the room to overflowing. Then, to the accompaniment of Kate's muted sobs came the gentle sounds of a newborn child, babbling softly in her father's ear. Never again would he neglect her. Not for his life. Not for anything.

Finally Francey was willing to let him go; Rick tucked her in and gave her a kiss. For a moment she seemed to smile, but it was fleeting, and she was off again. As he passed her desk, *Jane Eyre* caught his attention. He spent a moment, deciding, and then sat down. Carefully—even cautiously—he slid the book down the center of the desk until it was in front of him. And opened it.

Rick and Sally were living in the Village. They had been married for about two years, and though Rick was doing well, and they could have afforded a nicer place, they stayed where they were. Because Sally loved that apartment. Because Sally loved the Village.

"I see you finished *Jane Eyre*," Sally said, noticing that the book was back in its place on the shelf."

"Yeah," he said, noncommittally.

"So . . . Comments?"

"It was good. I liked it."

She went to him and put her arms around his neck. She kissed him.

"Come on," she said. "How'd you really like it?"

He sighed. "I loved it, okay? It was incredible. Are you satisfied now?"

Sally smothered his face with kisses, for one of the things she'd so loved about him was his decidedly un-macho taste in literature. "Yes," she said, "I'm satisfied now."

They held each other the way young lovers do when they've found that one other person on Earth with whom he and she are meant to spend the rest of eternity; and ten years later, and sitting at Francey's desk, Rick choked back a sob. He closed the book, and after carefully placing it in the exact spot that Francey had picked out for it, got back to work.

Rick returned the sun's gaze as it peered at him from somewhere beyond the East River. Though not a new sight to him, especially in recent weeks, today there was no frustration at its appearance because it marked the approach of the day that Lord Crimson would pass forever from his life. Rick sank blissfully into his recliner and closed his eyes, preparing to leave the world behind.

"Pop?"

With eyes remaining shut, he turned toward the direction of his daughter's voice. "Morning, sweetheart."

"G'morning. I forgot to tell you, Miss Gingery's taking us to the Met today."

"No kidding? You know, that museum is one of my favorite places in the whole world."

"Really, Pop?"

"Yes, really."

"Then maybe we could go together, sometime. Just you and me."

"I believe there's a distinct possibility that such an event could come to pass."

Rick was pretty much gone.

"Pop," she said, nudging him again.

He made an unintelligible sound.

"Can I borrow one of your sketch pads?"

Rick pointed in the general direction of his desk. "Check the middle drawer," he said, "and you'll also find a brand new box of pastels in there. It's yours."

Francey ran to the desk and pulled out the items she needed. Hugging them, she ran back and kissed her father.

"Thanks, Pop. I'm gonna draw you something really, really nice."

But Rick had already left the building.

Lizzie's class exited the underground station, and in a double line walked up the steps leading to the entrance of the great stone building. Francey, for the first time ever, was standing in front of the Metropolitan Museum of Art wondering how, in all the years of her young life, such a magnificent building could have escaped her notice.

The Met was unusually busy that day. A touring visit of Michelangelo's *Pietà* had arrived a few days earlier, and the line to get into the museum was stacked up around the block. Lizzie's class, their field trip having been arranged a month in advance, simply filed in. The place was a zoo. It was Grand Central Station at rush hour. Rush hour times ten.

The *Pietà*.—An introduction to a world inconceivable to these young minds jammed so full of the mindless claptrap that daily and relentlessly invaded their lives. Television, video games, Hollywood's spewed garbage. Here was an opportunity for Lizzie, not to mention Michelangelo, to steer them toward loftier heights than the gutter-high goals set for them by the media's merchants of chaos. And seemingly without incident, Lizzie and Alex shepherded the class, as it moved with the inexorable wave of bodies that flooded the museum, toward Michelangelo's incomparable masterpiece.

The line was long, and it moved slowly, but finally they were in front of it—the great sculptor's interpretation of the crucified body of Jesus, lying dead, in his mother's arms. Lizzie, Alex, the entire class stared, spellbound. Lizzie was enraptured. What a wonderful idea it had been. For everyone, that is, except Francey. From the moment the class had entered the museum, a voice, pleading and desperate, had called out to her. Left no choice but to find it, and hidden by the throngs, she'd immediately slipped away. From room to massive room she followed the urgent cries until, suddenly, the voice grew still. Its job—to bring the child home at last—was done. In awe, Francey looked around. She was standing, dead-center, in the Rembrandt Room.

Her eyes quickly swept the room and came to rest upon an old familiar memory. She sat down on a nearby bench and set about her task.

There wasn't nearly enough time for her to do justice to Rembrandt's entire masterpiece, so after doing a quick sketch, she zeroed-in on the nobleman's face. Blending, shading, texturing. And finally compensating for the faded colors that some three hundred-odd years of age had wrought. Her pastels moved like little sticks of lightning, and a crowd began to gather. They watched, dumbstruck, as beneath the fingers of the little girl, a work of art that rivaled anything in this room—the room with no rival in the entire museum—took shape. They were quiet, and spoke only in hushed tones so as not to disturb the child.

And the crowd grew larger.

Finally Alex had come back to Earth. A feeling grabbed him and he looked around. Instantly he was at Lizzie's side.

"Francey's gone," he said, his steady hands on her shoulders in an effort to keep her from panicking. "I know she's okay so far, but I need to find her fast." And Alex was gone also.

Lizzie was numb. Horrifying scenarios tried to make their way into her mind—but Alex was so certain. How could he know? She almost got down on her knees to thank God she had brought him along.

It was several years since last he had been in the Met, but it was as if it had been yesterday: that steel trap of a memory Lizzie so envied.

Quickly, and methodically, Alex wound his way through the museum. But the building was enormous, and it was taking too long. Any second now and it would be too late. Where would she have gone? He focused: the portrait she'd drawn of him; her use of light and shadow. He sprinted for the stairs.

The scream was heard throughout the museum—even as far away as the room in which Francey's class was gathered. Lizzie collapsed on the nearest bench. She grabbed hold of the nearest child and held onto her as if both their lives depended on it. And in her mind, she pushed Alex faster toward the terrified sound.

He rounded the top of the stairs; at the end of the long hallway lay his destination. Fueled by the screams, Alex fairly flew toward the Rembrandt Room, and once at the entrance, plowed mercilessly through what had become a solid mass of cultured rubberneckers. When at last he'd reached her she was standing on the bench, her arms outstretched, holding off the hordes. He grabbed her up and holding her tightly in his arms, whispered in her ear, "I'm here, Francey, I'm right here," and magically the screams and sobs quieted. She touched his cheek, and with calm but tear-filled eyes, said, "Don't be afraid, Edward. You're safe now. Safe in my arms." And after a few seconds more, and the present-day surroundings had come into focus, she said, with sort of a sheepish smile, "Oh, Alex . . . Hi."

"Hi," he said, and put her down.

"I guess I made a bit of a scene, huh?"

"Well, I guess you did, but who wouldn't, with a mob like this crowding you?"

"Right. Hey, where's my drawing?"

Alex surveyed the room. The crowd had backed off, and in a corner, a group holding Francey's pad was huddled together.

"Is that it?" Alex said, nodding in their direction.

"Yeah."

Hand-in-hand, they walked over to the group. The man

holding the pad looked up, a stupefied expression on his face. Alex eased the pad from his grasp.

"Sorry folks, the show's over," he said, and he and Francey turned on their heels and marched out of the room. The members of that select group watched them disappear around the corner, and then silently disbanded. Each of them had touched the exquisite work of art, and the miracle was part of them now. Their lives were changed forever.

Alex and Francey sat on the steps outside the museum. Lizzie, having gotten the agreement of one of the museum guards to watch her class, came rushing out.

"I just spoke to Rick and he's on his way. Alex'll stay with you 'til he gets here, but I need to get back inside to take care of the kids. Okay, sweetheart?"

Lizzie knelt down. She held her cheek to the little girl's and then kissed her. Really what she so desperately wanted to do was hold her, not letting her go for an instant until Rick had arrived; but there was the matter of her children. And after a moment's hesitation, went inside to tend to them.

Alex's curiosity was burning him up alive, but fearing, for Francey's sake, to venture too far into the realm of the unknown, he kept his questions to himself.

"Are you okay?" Francey said.

"Just trying to chill . . . and leave you alone."

"You don't have to leave me alone—and you don't have to worry about me either, okay? I'm fine. It's only when I'm right in the middle of it that it's painful."

"Then it's okay with you to talk about it?"

"Of course."

"Well I'm sure curious to know what happened in there, Francey, 'cause you scared the living daylights out of me."

Francey gave Alex her most comforting and reassuring look; not for all the world could she permit him to be distressed.

"Here's what happened," she said. "I was concentrating on my drawing for Pop and—uh oh, my pastels. I forgot them in the museum."

"Don't worry about it. I'll get you a new set."

"Okay." Francey took a breath. "Anyway, there I was, concentrating my brains out, and suddenly I got sucked back into one of my memories. So when I saw all those people crowded around me, I panicked because I thought they were coming to kill Edward."

Edward again.

"Francey," Alex said, delicately, "who is this Edward guy?"

"Edward Delaney. He was my lover. You know—back when I was Susan Sebastian."

"Susan Sebastian," Alex mused aloud, wondering at the name's familiarity.

"Anyway, as I was saying, I was trying to protect you from that mob—"

"Me? I thought you said Edward."

"You—Edward—same difference."

"What?"

"You don't remember yet," she said, "but you will. As soon as I figure out a way to jog your memory."

Suddenly, the sound of screeching tires. The cab door flew open and within seconds Rick was at their side. He sat down, and cradling Francey's head in his hands, pulled her close.

"Pop?" she said.

Rick's reply was to hold her tighter, while silently rocking her back and forth.

"I'm okay, Pop. I really am," she said, shifting her eyes—Rick's grasp, holding her head immobile—toward Alex. "See?—Me and Alex, just sitting here, shooting the breeze."

She seemed perfectly fine; he loosened his hold somewhat.

"Lizzie told me what happened."—Rick was talking to Alex.—"I don't know how I'll ever be able to show my gratitude."

"Don't sweat it, Mr. St. Michael. Francey's pretty special."

Rick grimaced at Alex's formality. "Would you mind calling me Rick?"

No, Alex wouldn't mind.

"Good. And your sister's undoubtedly got her hands full, so you should get back inside. And since I've had just about all the excitement I can handle for one day, we're going to take off."

"Bye, Alex," Francey said, as they all rose from the steps.

"Bye, guys. Guess I'll see you later."

Alex turned to head back into the museum. Rick and Francey waited until he'd disappeared through the great stone entrance and then, holding hands, they proceeded down the stairs and got into the waiting cab.

THE RESCUE

A S THE TAXI-DRIVER expertly maneuvered the cab in and out of traffic, Rick and Francey, typical New Yorkers that they were, remained oblivious to the ruckus that was going on outside. Blaring horns. Lewd gestures. Profanities, left and right. But no gunplay. That activity was reserved for Los Angeles. The land of the courteous driver.

Francey handed Rick the sketchpad. "It's for you, Pop."

It was a portrait he'd seen a hundred times before. Hanging in the Met. In countless art books he'd studied. The quick sketch she'd done of the entire painting, though hardly more than an outline, showed an attention to detail that couldn't have been more perfect. But the face. The eyes. The mouth. It was unfathomable.

"It's beautiful, sweetheart. Just beautiful. Thank you."

She smiled and leaned her head against her father's shoulder while he continued studying the work of art. Trying to understand. Then he saw it and shut his eyes to block it from his mind. It was signed—Susan Sebastian.

While he and Lizzie ate their take-out dinner—those thick Lo Mein noodles ordered from Hong Fat's Chinese restaurant in the Village—Alex related the conversation he'd had with

Francey outside the museum. With an emphasis on the part about Francey thinking that he had been Edward Delaney.

"And she was totally awake?" Lizzie said.

"Yeah."

"It just keeps getting curiouser and curiouser, doesn't it?" Lizzie said.

A few moments of silence, and then Lizzie spoke again. "I wish I'd seen the drawing. It was unbelievable, right?"

"I don't even have words."

"Yeah, I know," Lizzie said. "It was unbelievable."

"I was thinking," Alex said after another short silence, "that maybe Uncle Jules should be brought into the picture."

"I'm way ahead of you. I called him the morning after she drew your portrait. He's out of the country—off on another one of his campaigns, so naturally there's no way to get ahold of him. But according to his service, he's supposed to be getting back any day now."

"I haven't seen him since Dad's funeral," Alex said. "Remember his eulogy? The closing words? I swear to God, Lizzie, if I live to be a thousand, I'll never forget them—'Jonathan Gingery was unique to this world. There has never been another like him. There will never be another like him, and I mourn his loss more than that of any other soul I could ever know.'"

"Yeah," Lizzie said. "I remember . . ."

Having put the finishing touches on the presentation he and Johnny would be making the following evening, Rick took one final sip of coffee before calling it a night.

He peered into Francey's room. It was remarkable how much she resembled Sally when she slept. Tonight, for some reason, it struck him even more than usual causing a tightness in his throat that made it difficult to breathe.

He bent over her, intending to softly brush his lips across her forehead—and froze. It had just been a whisper, but the name seemed to echo throughout the room. Rick waited, praying. Her agitation was only slight; perhaps it would dissolve of its own accord. But then she said the name again, and Rick knew. Like no night-stalker Hollywood had ever conjured up, the dream was back, and if not stopped in its tracks would strike her down with every horrific weapon in its arsenal.

He used a gentle touch. "Francey, sweetheart, wake up." But his efforts had no effect. He shook her harder, his voice taking on a commanding tone, "Francey, wake up!" Still her cries worsened. He picked her up. Held her, comforted her, pleaded with her to wake up. To no avail.

Nearly out of his mind with panic, Rick rushed her into the bathroom. He ran a wash cloth under the freezing cold water and mercilessly soaked her face. No use.

Again and again he tried the washcloth with the same result while her screams, her sobs, and the sound of Edward's name seemed to shake the very foundation of the brownstone. There was only thing left to do, and with Francey clutched in his arms, he ran to the phone. He pushed the speaker button and then the speed-dial.

The sound of a phone ringing.

A click.

"Hello?" Lizzie said, wondering through a haze who was calling her at three o'clock in the morning.

"I can't wake her. She's in the middle of one of her memories and I can't get her out of it. Oh God, Lizzie, maybe Alex—"

"We're on our way."

Dial tone.

Lizzie's apartment, fortunately, was only a short distance from Rick's, both of them living in the vicinity of the school. Less than a minute from the time she'd hung up, she and Alex were standing at the curb hailing a cab. She jammed a hundred dollar bill in the driver's face and shouted the address at him. The cab burned rubber for a quarter of a mile.

Before the taxi had come screeching to a stop, the rear door was already open. The driver watched, with mild curiosity, as his two passengers tore up the stairs and through the entrance to the off-white brownstone. After they'd disappeared from sight, he drove off cheerfully and knocked off work. He'd already made his full night's wages.

Three flights to go.

Alex took the stairs, two and three at a time, while thoughts and pictures he didn't understand flashed through his mind. He pushed them aside; Francey's life was in his hands and there was time for nothing else.

A flight ahead of Lizzie, Alex crashed through the top-floor apartment door and grabbed Francey from Rick's outstretched arms. He shut his eyes and poured his soul into his voice. "I'm here, Francey. I'm right here. Just open your eyes and you'll see, okay?"

With Alex's mystical spell having been cast, the terror once again simply dissolved away. Then Francey opened her eyes and gazed lovingly at her young rescuer. "Edward," she said, "my sweet Edward. I thought they'd killed you. Oh, my darling . . ." And with an oh, so gentle touch, she caressed Alex's face. And drifted off.

The few moments of deathly silence were broken by Alex, hardly loud enough to nudge the peacefulness. "I guess I'll just go put her to bed."

Rick was numb, his bearings shot. He looked around for something familiar, something friendly. The couch appeared and he went for it, making it there just as his legs gave out. The implications of what might have happened, if not for Alex, sent a shock wave through him violent enough to tear a redwood out by its roots. And sobbing, he buried his face in his hands.

Lizzie went to him. She placed her body next to his, and after gently removing his hands from his face, she pulled his head to her. She said nothing. There were no words.

Rick was asleep. Careful not to disturb him, Lizzie stood up to stretch her legs. It was the first chance she'd had to look around his living room and something caught her eye. Having been lighted, at Francey's insistence, as if in a museum—overhead spotlights shining softly upon it—*Francey's Parthenon* seemed to call out, and Lizzie walked over to have a look. She smiled, seeing the title, and then she noticed an inscription in the upper left-hand corner.

> *For my daughter.*
> *I hope this will suffice.*
> *Love, Pop.*

Moved to tears by the beauty of the artwork and touched by the inscription, though its inside meaning escaped her, Lizzie, dreamily, found her way to Rick's bedroom. She lay down and as her eyes became accustomed to the darkness, the ceiling of the Sistine Chapel appeared in all its majesty, blanketing her in a whirlwind of emotions. Lizzie basked in those feelings for some time, thinking about tomorrow. What with all the commotion, she'd never had a chance to tell him. Where she was planning to take him. Whom she wanted him to meet. She smiled as she turned on her side preparing for sleep. Uncle Jules. It had been too long.

Rick opened his eyes. Through a haze he heard the sound of voices and clatter coming from the kitchen. He shook his head to clear it. What on Earth was going on?

He peered in. Francey and Lizzie were at the stove preparing his favorite breakfast—bacon and scrambled eggs. Alex was seated at the table, reading the paper, a cup of coffee in his hand. Lizzie turned away from the stove and smiling that radiant smile of hers, said, "Good morning, sleepyhead. Breakfast'll be ready in a minute."

Lizzie and her smile. It was the most beautiful thing Rick had ever seen. Everything was going to be all right, after all.

Someone was nudging his arm; he looked down to see Francey holding out a cup of coffee for him.

"Pop?"

"Yeah, sweetie. What's up?"

"Is it okay if I don't go to school today?"

"You know, I was actually going to suggest that very thing. I'm done with my project and after I drop it off we could hang out and do whatever you want."

"Or ..." Francey said, "Alex and I could go get me a new box of pastels, and you and Miss Gingery could go and do something together. And later, we could all hook up for coffee."

Rick looked at Alex.

"We were in such a hurry to get out of the museum," Alex said, "that we forgot Francey's pastels. I *did* promise to get her a new set."

He turned to Lizzie.

"I called in sick," she said. "There's somebody I want you to meet."

"Well," Rick said, "I hope nobody minds if we take a little time for me to drop some stuff off at the office."

"Sure, Pop," Francey said, patting his hand. "I think we can manage that."

"Here," Rick said, handing Alex a hundred dollar bill. "Pastels are pretty expensive, but there should be enough left over for you guys to get a nice lunch somewhere."

"That's okay," Alex said. "I'll take care of it."

"Take it. If you don't need it, you can give it back, but I'd feel better this way. Please."

"Okay. But no arguments later, right?"

"Right." And they shook on it.

Francey and Alex had left, leaving Rick and Lizzie working their way through yet another pot of coffee.

"So, this guy you want me to meet?" Rick said.

"Uncle Jules," Lizzie explained. "He finally got back from another one of his round-the-globe jaunts. Anyway, he was my father's oldest and dearest friend—a mutual interest in the Old Masters brought them together. Uncle Jules is arguably the world's foremost authority on pretty much anything art-related. As far as I'm concerned, though, it isn't even arguable. He's just the most amazing guy . . ."

She smiled at some pleasant reminiscences.

"He's not really my uncle," she said, picking up from where she'd left off, "but since Dad died, aside from Alex, Uncle Jules is the only other person in my life that I think of as family."

Lizzie reached her hands across the table. "Rick, listen to me. If there's anyone on the planet who can lend some insight into what's going on, it's Uncle Jules."

UNCLE JULES

ALERTED TO THE intruder by the jingling bell attached to the front door, Jules Steinholtz looked up from his studies. He growled. There were no appointments scheduled, and drop-ins were most unwelcome. He closed the enormous book and hoisted his eighty-five-year-old body out of the chair. He would make short work of his uninvited visitors.

Through the long corridors lined with floor-to-ceiling free-standing shelves he walked. The stacks of original artwork, signed and numbered prints, and priceless manuscripts went by unnoticed as he prepared himself for his first eviction of the week. He heard no voices. Good. Whoever it was appeared to be waiting in fear. His wrath was famous. He growled again.

With arms outstretched, she appeared at the end of the aisle; Uncle Jules' wrath dissolved to joy. And as they embraced, a silent pact was made: never again would either one permit so long a time to pass.

Lizzie pulled Uncle Jules by the arm over to where Rick was standing. "Uncle Jules," she said. "This is my friend, Rick St. Michael. Rick . . . Uncle Jules."

Uncle Jules looked with some wonder at the young man with whom he was shaking hands; for the first time in her life, Lizzie was allowing an outsider access to these hallowed halls.

"Come and sit down, children," the old man said, "and tell me to what I owe this indescribably delightful diversion."

In one corner of the room was a wonderfully ornate antique table. Uncle Jules and his guests made themselves comfortable in the magnificent, matching Victorian chairs. Chairs that countless museums had begged Uncle Jules to allow them to purchase. At any price. But these chairs, along with the table, had no price. A story we'll save for another time.

Lizzie lay the sketchpad down. Uncle Jules prepared himself, for he knew it would be a worthy offering; and with the same care he'd have taken with an original da Vinci, he opened it.

Looking upon the work of art for only but a moment, Uncle Jules closed his eyes in prayer. He was thanking God for having given unto him his friendship with Jonathan Gingery. Jonathan's daughter had always been a child to whom no other could hold a candle. But today she had gone one further. Today she had brought him a miracle.

His eyes met Lizzie's but he didn't ask, for if she were going to tell him of its origin, she'd have done so already.

He shifted his eyes toward the quiet young man across the table from her.

"I assume, Rick, that you have something to do with this."

"You could say so," Rick said, hesitantly. "At least, in a manner of speaking."

That he'd get no more from these two today was obvious, so he returned his attention to the drawing, this time in search of a signature. When he saw it, the result was electric. If it had been signed by Rembrandt himself, Uncle Jules would have been less unnerved. It was, of course, as impossible as the work of art itself.

"Wait here, children," he said, getting to his feet. "I'll be right back," and he took the long walk through the corridors and disappeared into the back room. When he returned, he was carrying a book. It was large, and old, and no doubt priceless. Gently he lay it on the table and took his seat again. He turned the pages, and when he'd found what he was looking for, Uncle Jules placed Francey's drawing side-by-side with the illustration open before him. From the desk drawer he took a magnifying glass.

"Come here, children, and have a look at this."

On either side of him, and looking over his shoulder, Rick and Lizzie studied what lay underneath the glass. A bold distinctiveness made the comparison simple. Two signatures, separated by more than three centuries, signed by the same hand. Numb, Rick and Lizzie sat down."

"I daresay, Elizabeth," Uncle Jules said, "there are few people in this world who know and appreciate you as I do. I remember, as if he were sitting across from me now, heated discussions with your father, each of us trying to outdo the other in the extolling of your virtues." He paused a moment, enjoying the memory. "That I have been rendered at a loss for words is a feat worthy of some note. That it was done at your hands, makes it, at least, bearable."

Lizzie was well aware that Uncle Jules' loss for words would be short lived, and she shot a warning look at Rick to hold on tight.

"I am not normally given to flights of fancy," the old man said, "so you must forgive me if I tell you that the existence of this work of art is simply not possible. You see, children, this is unquestionably an original Susan Sebastian. And though that in itself is remarkable beyond words, its significance is dwarfed when the question is put to us: how is it possible that Susan Sebastian—who last stood at an easel over three hundred years ago—was able to bring into creation a work of art barely a few days old?"

He waited a moment, letting his words sink in. As much for himself as for Rick and Lizzie.

"You're both familiar with the work of Rembrandt's represented here, are you not?"

They nodded.

"Yes, of course you are, and it's hanging in the Met for all to see. Now then—when we gaze with wonder upon that masterpiece, are we looking at the same painting that Rembrandt created? Sadly, no. Because—among other things—the colors have faded badly over the centuries. And so we are deprived of the miracle that Rembrandt truly was.

"My point is this," he continued. "These colors are so brilliantly executed, and so perfectly enhanced, as to stagger the imagination. If Rembrandt were alive today, he would be unable to improve on this."

The reverent silence that followed was finally broken, without disturbance, by a voice soft and melodious, conjuring sounds of the slow movement of a Schubert string quartet. "Do you know anything about her, Uncle Jules? About her life?"

"Hers was an existence too painful for me to dwell upon at any length," he said. "Susan Sebastian was a gift from Heaven. Beautiful in body and soul; and a talent, so extraordinary, as to defy comprehension. A tragic child who made the fatal error of falling in love with the wrong man."

Uncle Jules tended to his tears, while Lizzie pictured a despairing little girl.

"She was of the nobility, and the young man whom she loved was, alas, a commoner. The lad was killed by a local nobleman who had been promised her hand in marriage. Whether it was a duel of honor, or foul play, has never been determined—though murder would be my guess. After that, Lady Susan simply withered away. Her death, shortly there-after, dug an early grave for her father, consensus being that he played a role of some kind in the ghastly affair. And though much of this has been gleaned from conjecture, what remains steadfastly true is that the gift she possessed was one which doesn't often find its way to the surface of this planet."

"But why isn't she well known?" Lizzie said. "Even in Dad's huge collection of books, there's so little mention of her."

"Yes, and there exists no sadder fact than the forgotten memory of Susan Sebastian. That she passed this way at all was made known to me only by the wildest of coincidences, the circumstances of which are unimportant at the moment. The world has abandoned her, you see, because so little of her artwork survived her death. A few weeks before she died, she erected a funeral pyre and burned every last scrap of her work that she could lay her hands on; a task made simple by the fact that none of it ever left the grounds of the Sebastian estate. For some unknown reason, her father never allowed the sale of even one of her paintings. Perhaps he couldn't bear to part with anything wrought by his precious daughter's hands. I hope that was the case, for if it were otherwise, his sufferings in Hell would be made that much the worse."

"Do you know his name?" Lizzie said. "The man Susan loved, I mean."

"Ah, my dear. You are here to test the aging memory of an old man, is that it?"

Lizzie laughed. "You will no doubt and forever have the best memory of anyone I've ever known."

"Yes. Well. Let me think for just a moment. It was Edward. Edward . . . Started with a 'D,' I believe."

Rick and Lizzie exchanged glances. Uncle Jules had said enough to confirm the one character Jonathan's books hadn't been able to verify. Lizzie placed her hand over his. "You needn't search for it," she said. "It was Delaney. Edward Delaney."

Uncle Jules quit his struggle. Lizzie's ability to astonish him was, apparently, without limits.

"Yes, that's right," he said. "Delaney. I imagine it would do me little good to ask how you come by a bit of knowledge so arcane as to be privy to fewer than a handful of people on the planet."

"Give us a little time," she said. "Please."

Uncle Jules could wait. She would tell him soon enough. And if not, he would figure it out. Not that he would try, for he respected her desire for secrecy. But these things simply came to him.

"All right," he said. "But let me ask you this, since the two of you are so well informed. The villain in the story—his name refuses to loosen itself from the tip of my tongue. It was Bumble . . . or Crumble. Something in that ballpark, I'm quite certain."

Lizzie looked at Rick for permission. He nodded.

"It was Trumbull," she said. "Lord Randolph Trumbull."

Uncle Jules slumped back in his chair. "Oh that my good friend Jonathan were still with us. He'd have enjoyed this, isn't that right, darling?" And in that tiny moment, Lizzie and Uncle Jules shared a thousand memories.

Rick stood up. From all appearances, the business at hand had been concluded, and he was concerned about fielding any more awkward questions. He thrust his hand out. "Thank you, Mr. Steinholtz. I'm in your debt."

Uncle Jules stood up and took Rick's hand. "Please . . . I'm Uncle Jules . . . and if you are not yet aware of it, I'd like to be the one who brings it to your attention. You are an astonishing young man. Brought here, to these chambers, at Lizzie's side—that, in and of itself, is remarkable. But add to that the mystery which you have laid at my feet and the search for words becomes futile."

Uncle Jules placed his hand on the sketchpad. "May I hold onto this? For just awhile longer?"

"Of course," Rick said. "It's yours for as long as you want."

Rick and Lizzie walked down the hallway to the jingling sound of Uncle Jules' bell echoing in the background. It had turned eerie and ominous, and they quickened their pace, hoping to shake its haunting tintinnabulation.

"Prices sure have skyrocketed," Francey said, as she and Alex perused the hundreds of tubes of oil paints.

"I wasn't aware that you'd ever bought oil paints before."

"Surely you jest," she said, "but the cost of stuff didn't really mean much to me back in those days."

"Those days?"

"Yeah. You know. Back when—" She stopped. This was not exactly a topic for discussion in the middle of the hustle and bustle of a mega-art-supplies store. "Why don't we save this conversation for later?"

"Okay," Alex said. "But are you telling me that you know how to use oils also?"

"Of course, silly. Oils is actually my medium of choice. Except for when I'm on the go, like lately. 'Cause pastels are so handy and portable."

"Speaking of which," Alex said, "why don't we pick up what we came for and get out of here? There's this really cool little bistro that I know of . . ."

Seated at a sidewalk table outside the aforementioned bistro—a double cappuccino in front of each of them—Alex said, "You're sure it's okay with your dad for you to be drinking coffee?"

"Of course. I get one cup a week, and since this is actually the first cup I've had in at least two weeks, I'm entitled to two cups today—technically speaking."

"I'm not sure Rick would agree with that."

Francey giggled. "I'm just kidding, silly."

God he loved her calling him that.

Francey pulled her new box of pastels from her backpack and opened it up. "These are just perfect," she said, gently caressing the little chalk-like pieces.

"Francey," Alex said, feeling like he was about to tread on dangerous ground, "Can I ask you something?"

"You may ask whatever your heart desires."

"Okay," he said. "Here's the question: this drawing ability of yours.—Where'd it come from?"

"Well, let's see," she said. "Lots of places. And lots of teachers. But if you want to know who my favorite and most influential teacher ever was—it was Rembrandt."

Why was it he felt not even the slightest bit disturbed at these words? So what if Rembrandt lived three hundred and fifty years ago? The Old Master's influence on Francey's artwork would have been obvious to any second-year art student, and since, according to Rick, she'd never before shown even a passing interest in art of any form, how else would she have picked it up?

"Anyway," Francey continued, "I was already pretty accomplished by then, and I can't really remember who I studied with before him—just too long ago, I guess. But after Rembrandt I remember perfectly, and my second most influential teacher, I'd have to say, was Monet."

"Wow. No kidding?" Alex said. "That was like over two hundred years later."

"Yeah, that's right. Rembrandt was alive during the sixteen hundreds and Monet was around in the late eighteen and early nineteen hundreds. Hey, I'm pretty impressed that you knew that."

"Yeah. I'm actually fairly well informed—about art and art history. Because of my dad."

"Cool. We should talk sometime."

"I seriously doubt that I could keep up with you."

"Don't be sil—" She skidded to a stop and her eyes lit up like a full moon on a pitch-black night. "Man, oh man, oh man—I just got the most incredible idea."

She pulled the sketchpad out of her backpack.

"What are you doing?" Alex said.

But her pastels were already moving and she said, without looking up, "Shhh, I'm concentrating."

This time, no force on Earth could have distracted her. So focused was she, that had an earthquake split the ground beneath and sucked her into its chasm, it would have gone unheeded. Francey, at last, had realized how to get Alex to remember. And not throughout all the decades and centuries had anything been half so important. The task before her was clear. Perfection alone was not enough. It had to live. It had to speak.

In wonderment Alex watched as Francey's concentration seemed to lead him by the hand into a world of their own making; a world whose entrance could be gained by them, but not another living soul.

Finally satisfied, Francey tore the page from her sketchpad, and handling this masterpiece as if it were a child's first attempt at drawing stick figures, she handed it to Alex.

"Recognize her?" she asked.

Not having felt rushed, as she had in the museum, the time and effort necessary to do her subject justice had been taken. Alex, as he stared at the portrait, felt like he was losing his grasp on reality. It was a drawing on sheet of paper, but it was alive. He heard her voice, her laughter, her tears; and it was as if they had never been apart. He put his cheek to hers and felt her breath, warm and sweet. And clear as a crisp autumn afternoon when the chill of winter first peeks over the horizon, her love for him was whispered in his ear.

"This is . . . Susan Sebastian," Alex said, finally able to take his eyes from the portrait.

It had worked. Inside, Francey was aglow, but she restrained her joy because Alex was badly shaken. So she spoke gently and with just a hint of satisfaction. "Well, technically speaking, it's me. But Susan Sebastian was my name at the time."

For a welcome change, the heat of the sun had broken through the clouds. It was having a warming effect on the streets of New York; and Rick and Lizzie, taking advantage of it, had leisurely walked the considerable distance from Uncle Jules' archives to the coffee shop across from the school. There had been few words exchanged, but it didn't matter, because at the moment most topics had lost their significance. What did matter, however, was the quiet comfort in their closeness.

They had a few minutes yet before Francey and Alex were due to meet them, and Lizzie and Rick were quietly nursing a couple of double cappuccinos.

"I'd say you've done quite well in the cast of characters you've chosen to surround yourself with," Rick said, breaking a several minutes-long silence.

"You mean Uncle Jules?"

"Yeah, and your dad, too."

"How do you know about my father?"

"Little things I've picked up here and there. A couple of things Francey's mentioned to me. And today, Uncle Jules— the reverence in his voice when he spoke of his good friend Jonathan."

She smiled, but there was a bleakness to it. Uncle Jules' and Jonathan's friendship had been of a sort that would continue on long after they both had left this Earth. But until their paths crossed again on the next plane of existence—aside from Jonathan's two children—Uncle Jules would miss him most of all. Lizzie cast her eyes forlornly down and lapsed into a silent sadness. Rick understood only too well how much she missed her father, and after struggling to come up with something that would bring her back home, he said, "I left one out."

Puzzled by what he meant, Lizzie looked up.

"One member of your heroic cast of characters," Rick said, "namely, your little brother. Do you realize that a few days ago it would have been inconceivable to me that I'd have felt safe leaving Francey in the care of a teen-aged boy? And now, here I am feeling more comfortable knowing she's with Alex than with anyone else on the planet. And that includes me, for God's sake."

"Yeah . . . Alex," Lizzie mused. "He does break the mold, doesn't he?"

"Listen, Lizzie," Rick said, steeling himself. "About last night—you and Alex—and the nightmare . . . I just want you to know how much I—" But as desperate as he was to thank her for her part in saving Francey's life, still he was unable to work his way through the emotional overwhelm, and was forced to say, choking on the words, "I'm sorry. It'll have to wait 'til later."

Lizzie reached over with her comforting hands. "I swear to you," she said, "everything's going to be okay." And as she made that vow, she added one more man to her astonishing cast of characters.

"There they are," Francey said, as she and Alex walked into the coffee shop. And unnoticed, they ambled on over.

"Hi guys," Alex said.

"Oh, what a couple of little sneaks," Lizzie said, disentangling her hands from Rick's.

"Okay, here's what's happening," she said, as Alex and Francey sat down.

"Rick's gotta go home to change for his presentation, and Francey—you're going to come home with me and Alex. We'll hang out and have dinner, and Rick'll come over to pick you up after his meeting. How does that sound?"

"Sounds wonderful," Francey said.

And Alex said, while handing Rick his hundred dollar bill, "See? Didn't need it."

Rick nodded and put it back in his wallet.

LORD CRIMSON

RICK, WEARING A sport coat and semi-dressy slacks, about as dressed up as he ever got, stepped off the elevator on the top floor of the Plaza Hotel. This was the last time he'd ever have to see, hear, or even think about Lord Crimson again, but the relief he should have been feeling was, instead, a profound sadness. Dwelling on it for a moment, he chalked it up to misplaced emotions due to events of late; he shook it off and prepared himself. Though lying in wait was a pressure-cooker situation that would have sent most men scurrying for the hills, it was with a dead-steady hand that Rick knocked on the door.

A few moments later, Mr. Portico opened the door. "Mr. St. Michael, I presume," he said, and after doing a fast but thorough inspection, gave to Rick his silent approbation.

"Yes, that's right," Rick said, offering his hand. "How do you do?" It was a phrase he didn't often use, but it seemed to fit tonight's occasion.

Mr. Portico, momentarily taken aback by this blatant disregard for propriety, recovered himself nicely, and taking Rick's hand with a firm grip, introduced himself, adding, "His Lordship and Mr. Falstaff are awaiting your arrival in the conference room. If you'll be so kind as to follow me . . ."

A few steps behind the butler, Rick walked into the most expensive hotel suite in all of New York City. Mr. Portico led the way to the conference room where Johnny and Lord Crimson were getting to their feet to greet him. Johnny made the introductions, and they sat down.

"Mr. Portico," Lord Crimson said. "If it's not too much trouble—some refreshment for Mr. St. Michael, please. A straight up martini with two olives, if I'm not mistaken."

"Ordinarily, that'd be right, sir," Rick said, "but tonight, if you don't mind, just some water will be fine."

Mr. Portico returned with Rick's water and placed it on the table as gently as if it had been a Fabergé egg. And just as deftly, Johnny's and Lord Crimson's empty glasses were replenished, after which Mr. Portico withdrew.

With a subtle nod, Rick gave Johnny the go-ahead; Johnny placed the portfolio on the table. He removed a large folder and slid it to Lord Crimson.

Lord Crimson shut his eyes and, with all his strength, mustered an attempt to banish the only glimmer of hope he'd ever allowed himself to feel; the crushing disappointment, otherwise, would have been, at best, unbearable.

That done, he opened the folder.

Then he opened his eyes.

For a minute or more, he didn't move. For a minute or more, he didn't make a sound. And such was the silence in the room that the plop of the teardrop, falling upon the drawing, was audible. Lord Crimson took a handkerchief from his pocket and blotted dry his tears. He spent one more fleeting glance on the illustration and turned to Rick.

"I've always known," he said, "that somewhere there existed a man able to do what you have done. When Mr. Falstaff was kind enough to meet with me two months ago, he said some things which allowed me an indulgence I had never before permitted into my world: hope.

Lord Crimson faltered and was again forced to use his handkerchief.

"I didn't know myself what it would look like," he said, "but this astonishing work of art has caused it all to fall into place; for every brick, every shingle, every blade of grass and flower—is exactly where it should be."

And then Lord Crimson asked the question against which Rick had been bracing himself: "How did you do it? How could you have known?"

In silence, Rick returned Lord Crimson's searching gaze. An honest answer, something which would open his daughter up to exposure and scrutiny, would never pass his lips.

"I'm sorry," he said. "Please understand that I have my reasons."

Lord Crimson's eyes remained on Rick. He wouldn't push it, for it wasn't his style, but he needed, at least, a thread on which to hang. "Perhaps at some later date?" he said. It was as close to groveling as Lord Crimson had ever come in his life.

Rick tried to envision the circumstances under which he would be willing to reveal the truth. It was inconceivable. Unanswerable questions would have to be answered. And a nightmare like no other would have to be disassembled, bit by bit, with each piece then shattered beyond repair. In his mind, Rick threw up his arms in despair. But what was the point in crushing Lord Crimson's hopes entirely? After all, anything's possible. And thus he said, with hope injected, "I pray for that day, sir. For my sake—as well as yours."

Lord Crimson took solace in this and raised his glass. "To Crimson Manor."

After saying good night to Francey, Lizzie went to join Alex in the kitchen. She poured herself a cup of coffee and sat down. "Well," she said, having suspected for hours that Alex had been waiting until they were alone so that he could drop another bombshell. "I'm listening."

"Okay," Alex said. "I'll be right back."

After retrieving the drawing from its hiding place on the top shelf of his closet, Alex placed it face down on the kitchen table.

"I need to warn you," he said. "No matter what you've already seen, there's no way you're gonna be prepared for this." And he turned it over.

The reaction was instantaneous. Lizzie's heart froze in mid-beat, and as if her lungs had been flattened by a sledge-hammer, she gasped. With trembling fingers she caressed the sheet of paper and a shiver ran through her bones; she had just touched the living flesh of Susan Sebastian. Alex watched as his sister's head shook in disbelief. He listened to her say, with a reverence he'd never before heard from her lips, "I've never seen anything half so beautiful." And just in time she set the drawing aside so that her tears would fall on the bare tabletop.

"Yeah, I know," Alex said. "And there's more. So get ready, because it's kind of fantastic."

But there was no need for her to prepare herself, because at that moment, Lizzie would have believed anything her little brother had chosen to say.

"That's Susan Sebastian," Alex said. "I guess you've already figured that out, but I just like saying the name. Now, listen to this: Francey's been trying to come up with a way to get me to remember—you know, the seventeenth century—her and me, together? So she drew that portrait in the hopes that it would jog my memory. I mean, there we were, just sitting outside the bistro, and she drew that . . . You know, I want to call it a masterpiece, but even that doesn't do it justice."

"No," Lizzie murmured. "There's no word for it."

A few days ago the question would have been fantasy. But those few days were now an eternity, and Lizzie asked, "Did it work? *Do* you remember?"

"Are you asking me that seriously? You don't think Francey and I are both completely out of our minds?"

"No . . . So? Do you?"

"Yeah, I do. I don't remember everything that Francey does, but I sure remember Susan Sebastian. Just like I'd last seen her yesterday."

Rick's familiar knock sounded at the front door, and the sparkle that instantly chased away the dazed look in his sister's eyes didn't go unnoticed. Lizzie turned the drawing face down and listened to the approaching footsteps. The sound stopped, and she turned in her chair.

"Hi," Rick said.

"Hi," she said. "So, how'd it go?"

"Pretty much as expected. May I see Francey's latest masterpiece?"

Lizzie looked at him questioningly.

"The radio in the cab," he explained. "It's all over the news. Apparently there are two shots—one of Alex and one of the drawing. Nothing showing Francey's face though, thank God."

"You'd better sit down for this," Lizzie said, and as she turned the drawing face up, the phone rang. The conversation was one-sided. Lizzie, silent until the end, said, "Okay, I'll talk to Rick and call you back. There's a couple of things you need to be made aware of."

Quietly she hung up the wall phone and sat back down.

"Rick?" she said.

Lost in the drawing, he had hardly been aware that the phone had rung. Without looking up, he murmured something.

"That was Uncle Jules."

"Yeah?" he said, crashing back to the planet's surface.

"He saw Alex's picture on the news. He wants us to come to his office tomorrow. He said . . . 'Bring the little girl.'"

Rick lowered his eyes; his heart lay crushed beneath a boulder. Lizzie touched his hand. "Listen to me . . . please. There isn't an ill-intentioned bone in Uncle Jules' body. And if there's anyone who can help . . ."

He looked up and saw that concern for him and Francey had glossed damply across her eyes; it gave him strength. "Listen, guys," he said, "it's kind of late. I'm gonna go get Francey and take off."

"Why don't you leave her here?" Lizzie said. "She's fast asleep and we're just going to be getting together in the morning again, right?"

"Yeah," Rick said. "Not to mention the fact that she's probably better off here, with you guys, than with me, anyway."

"You want to know what I think?" Alex said, immediately upon Rick's departure.

"Not particularly," Lizzie said, noting the devilish look in his eye.

"I think you're smitten."

"I'm quite sure I said I didn't want to know what you think."

"You *do* realize that we saw you guys—you know—with your hands wrapped around each other's."

"Francey saw?"

"Yeah. You wanna know what she said to me?"

"Why must you insist on going through this ritual of asking my permission when you're just going to tell me anyway?"

"She said, wouldn't it be great if Pop and Miss Gingery got together?"

Lizzie, despite her best efforts, smiled. "You kids are such little sneaks. I'm going to bed."

As she reached the kitchen door, Lizzie turned. "He *is* something, though, isn't he?" she said, and still smiling, she headed for bed.

THE TRUTH

HE LIGHT IS dimmed; her portrait lies at his side. Myriads of churning thoughts run rampant through his mind, 'til suddenly a voice cries out to him, stilling all else nearby. He lifts her up and holds her heart to his; and as their syncopated heartbeats mesh, two lovers set sail upon a sea of tenderness which could only have existed in a dream.

The year is 1665. Riding through the now familiar English countryside is nineteen-year-old Edward Delaney. In the distance he spies a young girl standing at an easel. His curiosity is aroused, for here, without the accompaniment and protection of a lady-in-waiting, is a high-born young lady. Such independence is unheard of, and he rides closer. Once able to discern her features his curiosity begins to smolder for up until that moment he'd have sworn that a creature this beautiful existed only in fairy stories. And since making a friendly nuisance of himself never fails with the young girls in his village, Edward stops his horse directly in her line of sight. The fifteen-year-old Susan Sebastian, however, is not so easily amused.

"Move aside, sir," she says. "You are blocking my view."

A different approach is clearly needed; Edward rides around to her back, while Susan ignores this impudent boy who actually has the effrontery to now be looking over her shoulder.

It is with a discerning eye that Edward studies Susan's painting, for his father, a parish priest, had been diligent in ensuring that his son's education in reading, writing, and the arts wasn't lacking. The unearthly beauty of her artwork, combined with the young noblewoman's breathtaking loveliness leaves Edward no choice but to continue making a nuisance of himself. We must forgive him, for it's the only way he knows.

"Not bad," he says. "Perhaps your perspective could use some work, but you must not concern yourself with such trivialities. A keener eye will come with practice."

"Sir," Susan says, "it would appear that your eyesight, rather than my perspective, is what is in need of improvement; and if only a shred of decency resides within you, you will remove yourself from this place. And as there may be a remote possibility that I will someday pass this way again, I implore you never to return."

Drastic measures are definitely in order here, and an idea strikes him. It's new, and novel, but given the situation, necessary. He dismounts and walks to her side. And speaks the truth.

"Forgive me . . . please. If you will but cast your eyes in my direction, you will discover that I no longer play the fool from whom you wish yourself to be rid. As for your painting, I am not ignorant in these matters and thus can scarcely believe this work of art was done, not by an old master, but by a young noblewoman." Edward pauses, gathering his courage. "A young . . . and very beautiful noblewoman."

Susan can't help turning toward him, and as she finally looks upon his face—his handsome, sensitive, cheerful face—she softens, and melts.

"I forgive you," she says, "and should you choose to return tomorrow, I will paint your portrait."

"Til tomorrow then," Edward says, while mounting his horse. "May I ask your name?"

"I am Lady Susan Sebastian."

"I am pleased to make your acquaintance, Milady. And I am Edward Delaney."

Susan's admiring gaze follows the figure of the boy as he rides off into the distance. He's gone from sight now, but her look yet lingers. And she wonders—what is this sensation burning deep within her breast?

Alex awoke, the eyes through which he looked at the world, changed forever. It was a memory. Just like Francey's.

Careful to leave Francey's sleep undisturbed, Lizzie got out of bed. After showering, starting a pot of coffee percolating, and placing the makings for breakfast on the counter, she went back to her room and sat down on the bed. She placed her hand lightly on Francey's shoulder and the little girl opened her eyes to Lizzie's quiet smile.

"Hi," Francey said, wondering what she was still doing there.

"It was my suggestion for you to spend the night here," Lizzie said. "It seemed like a needless bother to wake you just to take you home since we were all getting together this morning anyway."

"Okay . . . But how come we're getting together? I mean, it's fine—I just didn't know about it."

"We decided while you were asleep."

Lizzie then told her about Uncle Jules: of his unmatched knowledge of all things art; of the immense respect afforded him by the art world at large; and of how he had expressed an interest in meeting her.

"Cool," Francey said. But she had her mind on something else. Something of a more personal nature. Hesitatingly, she lay her hand on top of Lizzie's.

"I told Pop about that conversation we had the other day—about how similar you and your dad, and me and Pop were, remember?"

"Yes, I remember."

"He said that means we must be really good friends. You know—to be so comfortable with each other's company that we can talk about such intimate things. Was he right?" Francey asked. "Are we friends? I mean . . . good friends?"

"My sweet child," Lizzie said, taking Francey's hand and holding it to her lips. "We're best friends."

Alex was at the table, already well into the pot of coffee his sister had started brewing. Cobwebs due to participation in a fairy tale were impeding his progress toward fully waking up.

"Morning, sweetie," Lizzie said.

The cup to his lips, Alex rolled his eyes.

"Hey," she said. "Rough night?"

Feeling Francey's presence behind him, Alex shoved aside his unacceptable behavior and said, "Just a few cobwebs. No need for concern." Then he gave Francey his best smile, and the one she gave him in return sent the cobwebs merrily on their way.

Rick, having arrived and breakfast having been served, lay the morning paper on the table and said, "Perhaps there's some interest here in a news item that doesn't deal with death, pestilence, war, or starvation."

"Sure, Pop. Let's see."

He opened the paper—a full page from the *New York Times* devoted to two photographs. The first was an excellent shot of Alex watching a little girl drawing a picture. The second—a close-up of the portrait. Printed on magazine quality paper, the color photos were a triumph of newsprint clarity. The caption?—*Little Miss Rembrandt.*

"Wow," Francey said. "Great shot of you, Alex."

"Yeah, right . . . thanks," Alex muttered, kicking himself for not having noticed the nearby photographer.

"Sweetheart," Rick said, in a tone of voice she didn't often hear. "I want you to do something for me, okay? No more drawing in public. People just aren't ready for it."

"Okay, Pop," she said, patting his hand. "You're the boss."

Jingling to beat the band, Uncle Jules' door opened. The Gingerys and St. Michaels filed in to find him, seated at his beautiful antique table, awaiting their arrival. He stood, his eyes seeking Alex; whereupon the young boy went to the old man, and as if they had been father and son long parted, they embraced.

Next, Uncle Jules turned to the little girl. "Hello, Francey," he said. "I'm Uncle Jules."

"Francey St. Michael," she said, putting out her hand.

As they shook hands, the old man added, quietly, "I'm deeply honored."

"From what I've heard," Francey replied, "I believe the honor is mine."

Moved, and even humbled, by words from a child. Someone, perhaps, to share that special place in his heart, which had been Lizzie's exclusive domain for so long.

He turned to Lizzie. "Twice in but two days. My poor heart threatens to burst with joy."

They hugged, and kissed, and then Uncle Jules locked Rick in his sights. "I told you yesterday, did I not, that you were an astonishing young man? Behold, children, for the proof is nigh."

He indicated for all to make themselves comfortable and the chairs were quickly filled. Lizzie took the sketchpad from her oversized purse, and opening it to the portrait, slid it to Uncle Jules.

As he cast his eyes deeply into the soul of Lady Susan Sebastian, Uncle Jules realized just how futile his effort to prepare himself had been, for in his grasp was a work of art beyond the scope of anything he'd ever seen. He raised his eyes to the little girl's and wondered how it came to be that such a child had made her home upon so ordinary a planet. Steadying himself against the table, the old man stood up.

"Please excuse us," Uncle Jules said. "Francey and I have a few things to discuss," and he put his hand out to her.

Francey got to her feet, and Lizzie, afraid Rick might protest, touched his arm. He relaxed, and they watched as Uncle Jules and Francey disappeared beyond the long corridors. The click of the shutting door broke the silence, only to echo and fade away. The sound had been oddly comforting and each wished for another to end the quietness. One minute later, someone did.

"Guys?" Alex said, his voice, a soft clap of thunder.

Rick and Lizzie turned their wide-open, unblinking eyes toward him, both thinking the same thought. What astoundment now, Alex?

"Last night," he said, "I met Susan Sebastian."

There was a magical something about the far-off land of Edward Delaney and Susan Sebastian, for just as Francey's audience had been, so too was Alex's swept away; captivated throughout the telling and up until the very end when Alex wrapped it up by saying, "And so the next day Susan painted Edward's portrait, and the rest, as they say . . . Well, you know."

"What do you suppose happened to that painting?" Lizzie said.

Alex steadied himself before replying, "It was buried with Susan."

"But how could you know that, sweetheart? How?"

He replied only with the water in his eyes. And through that wetness Alex watched as Rick cast his own eyes sadly down upon the floor; and Alex's heart was stung, yet even more than by the memory.

"Don't you see, Rick?" he said, using the gift of succor that had been given to him in almost the abundance it had been given his sister. "It's what Francey wanted—to remind me of who we were."

There followed no barrage of questions, nor skeptical remarks. It had become all too evident that Alex and Francey belonged to a special group of uplifted souls whose presence here on Earth couldn't be explained. The right to question it belonged to no one. And for several minutes more the stillness remained undisturbed. Then—

"We're back, guys," Francey said, and the storybook feeling surrounding Uncle Jules' table dissolved, returning everyone to the planet's surface. And where had they been? Perhaps in the clearing beneath the mighty oak, enjoying a cup of tea with the young lovers.

"There now. Not too painful, I trust," Uncle Jules said.

"Uncle Jules," Francey said, "has the most incredible collection of books I've ever seen, and I can come over and look at them anytime, right?"

"Anytime, darling. Anytime at all."

To Alex, Uncle Jules said, "My boy—would you consider it a terrible imposition if I asked you to keep Francey company in the back room—just for a short while? There's lots of great stuff I know she'd love to show you."

And though no one had more right than he did, to hear what Uncle Jules had to say, Alex nodded agreeably and said, "C'mon, Francey, let's go take a look at those books."

Uncle Jules waited for the sound of the closing door.

"I apologize deeply for the ordeal that I have put you through," he said to Rick, "but I had to see for myself . . . to understand how such a thing could be."

The silence of a tomb would have been deafening, if compared with Uncle Jules' chambers at that moment.

"Do you remember," Uncle Jules asked of Lizzie, "what most fascinated Jonathan about Rembrandt?"

Today Lizzie would find it more difficult than usual to speak of her father. If only he could have known how badly she needed him.

"Of course," she said. "His use of light and shadow."

"Yes. I know you remember. I didn't mean to question your memory, sweetheart."

Lizzie nodded; her sadness, heart-wrenching.

"And you also know that there has never been anyone who has even approached the mastery which he achieved in that regard. That is . . . until now."

Uncle Jules placed his hand on Francey's drawing, and the loving warmth emanating from Susan Sebastian flowed into the very fiber of his being. His next words, spoken as if in a grand cathedral praying to the angels of Heaven, were these:

"My children, listen to me. There's but one way Francey could have acquired the skills with which to create such a monumental work of art. And if you haven't yet surmised it, then hear these words as you have heard no others. Francey, and Susan Sebastian . . . are the same person."

ENLIGHTENMENT

THE SUNLIT TRUTH rocketed across the clear, blue skies, scattering to kingdom come the more than three hundred years of accumulated storm clouds. This fantastic notion had, so many times, skipped lightly through Lizzie's thoughts, but it had been looked upon as folly and instantly discarded; for in this world of sanity and reason, a plausible explanation had to be found. But such was no longer the case. There were truths, universal in nature, that stood out above all others. And above even those, stood this: from Uncle Jules lips, only gospel was spoken.

Quickly Lizzie turned to Rick. To lend support should it be needed. And as she did, she felt his hands close around hers; for his thoughts were of her, as hers were of him. She wondered, could her emotions run any deeper?

Together they gave their attention back to Uncle Jules who sat silent and motionless as a ghost ship becalmed. Watching, waiting, and thanking God for having had the wisdom to send these innocent and trusting children to him.

"All right," he said, once their attention was again his. "While Rembrandt's influence on Francey is obvious, there is yet another influential hand at work, though it is subtle. Care to venture a guess as to whose it is?" Uncle Jules said, as he handed the drawing to Lizzie.

Lizzie's eye was truly well trained in these matters, and though she hadn't noticed it before, looking at it now, from Uncle Jules' guiding perspective, there did appear to be something—so subtle, yet so utterly intertwined in every masterful nuance of the portrait.

"Monet?" she said. She knew, now, and nothing would ever seem impossible to her again.

The old man smiled. "You, my dear, are indeed your father's daughter. It is undeniably Monet, and it is his added influence which gives Francey's artistry an other-worldliness that, heretofore, has not been seen on this planet. The child is truly a divine miracle."

Uncle Jules took a handkerchief from his pocket, and as if he were blotting the newly-written signature of an Old Master, he dried his tears.

"Though should the entire world take up arms and declare that I be put to death for lunacy and witchcraft, still my precious Lizzie would remain at my side, taking me at my word, and defending me even with her life." He smiled fleetingly at her, and turned his attention.

"I'm not so presumptuous as to expect the same of you, Rick, so I simply ask that you hear me out.

"No stone has been left unturned in the quenching of my thirst for knowledge regarding the man whom I consider to be the greatest of the Old Masters; and for quite some time, I have rested secure in the knowledge that there exists no one more expert on the subject of Rembrandt than I. I tell you this, not to boast, but to put into perspective what I'm now about to say. Francey's knowledge, though of a different sort, dwarfs mine in comparison. Hers is of an intimate and personal nature, common only to those who have strolled arm-in-arm through the countryside, or broken bread at the dinner table while discussing the events of the day."

Uncle Jules went on to tell them of Francey's detailed description of Rembrandt's studio; his meticulous treatment of his paints; the precise placement of his easel with regard to the time of day and the position of the sun; and of her reverent imagery of priceless artwork, hung lazily on the walls, and stacked carelessly in the corner.

"Much the way a teacher explains to a favorite student," Uncle Jules said, "she described for me his method of blending colors, and demonstrated how he held his brush. Then, by guiding my hand in the same manner Rembrandt had guided hers, she showed me how he had instilled in her the greatness that we see before us today. And while her little hand held mine, I was transported to a place I could never have imagined I'd visit. And if there yet remains a doubt, let this cast it aside. It is not a secret that when Rembrandt painted he often mumbled to himself. But the content of those mumblings has forever remained unknown. Unimportant, you say? Perhaps . . . in the grand scheme of things. Nevertheless, today I was made privy to what those silly utterances were. And why do I assume the truth of Francey's words? Simple enough. She spoke them, not in English, but in Flemish—Rembrandt's native tongue."

"Flemish?" her father said, soft as wrung-out church bells, dying away.

Uncle Jules' eyes passed gently over Rick, allowing him, in an instant's time, to feel the enormity of the old man's love and understanding.

Then, with the certainty of a man whose teachings stemmed only from that which he knew for himself to be true, Uncle Jules said, "And now children, you will learn how such a thing could come to pass." And the beating of three hearts seemed to echo through the rafters.

"My interests," Uncle Jules said, "which are considerable in number, originate with a passion for the Old Masters that is all consuming. This has always been so, and I've spent a goodly portion of my life in the pursuit of discovering just what it is that sets those men apart from the rest of humanity. That I was able to discover the truth is a testament to the fortitude of the human spirit; though I'll spare you the painful details of how I made the discovery, for it would take some time to relate. Let it suffice to say that my search has carried me to every corner of the globe into places, so far off the beaten trail, you would find it difficult to believe they exist.

"And so, here it is.—The true nature of man is not that he is a body, but a spirit—an *essence of being* is the way in which I think of it—distinct and individual from all others, and merely using the body as a temporary place of residence. It is a quality—an awareness—which we all possess, or to put it more accurately—which we all *are*—from the lowliest dregs of humanity, to the most uplifted among us. It is only the size—the majesty—of the spirit that differs from individual to individual. In other words, we don't live only one time. Nor twice. Nor even three times. The *being* residing within our bodies is immortal and thus experiences lifetime, upon lifetime, upon lifetime. For most of us, the past is inaccessible and lies dormant . . . useless. But there are some, though they be few in number, who are able to call upon these encounters of yore. Mozart, for example, was barely out of his infancy when he composed his first symphony. Michelangelo sculpted the *Madonna of the Stairs* while still a teenager. At his concert debut, Jascha Heifetz turned the world of violin playing on its ear. He was barely ten years old.

"Men such as these, as well as the Old Masters, born somehow with the ability to build upon their learnings from generations past, still lacked the one thing that sets Francey apart from any I've yet heard of. And that is—the child has vivid recollections of that which the rest of humankind has long forgotten. And though this is a gift unfathomable by earthly estimations, it is no doubt responsible for her nightly turmoils of late."

Though shaken to the core by Uncle Jules' words, Rick's fear for Francey's life now overwhelmed all else. And when he spoke, his hopelessness wrung Uncle Jules' soul without mercy. "But what are we to do . . . about the dreams?"

"What's critical for all of us to understand," Uncle Jules said, "is that these are actual memories of a time so fraught with despair as to make us wonder that she has endured them as well as she has. The one thing of which I am certain is this—somehow the child has begun a search and no matter the cost, she cannot give it up. The key to what or whom she seeks lies within the dream itself, and you may rest assured that once discovered, its power will be broken. But it must be found quickly, children, for just as it has no doubt plagued her for centuries, so shall this horror continue to wreak its havoc on into eternity."

"Maybe the key lies with Alex," Rick said.

"Alex?" The old man questioned.

Buried in grief, Rick looked to Lizzie for help. She nodded and took over.

"There seems to be an unusually close connection between Alex and Francey," she said, "even though they only met for the first time a few days ago. Because now, all of a sudden, Alex is having these same . . . memories."

"I'm not surprised," Uncle Jules said. "We go through life making friends, and sometimes a friendship is so strong, so indestructible, that although it is unbeknownst to us, we continually seek that same person out. To learn that Francey and Alex have crossed paths countless times over the generations wouldn't surprise me in the slightest."

"So the two of them being thrown together like this isn't just some astronomically wild coincidence?"

"Coincidence?" Uncle Jules chuckled. "Hardly. In fact, if they had gone much longer *without* finding each other . . . That, my dear—astronomically speaking—would have been far wilder."

A CHANGE OF PLANS

THE BOEING BUSINESS Jet taxied down the runway at Kennedy International Airport. On board, nursing a martini, Lord Crimson stared absently out the window. What was this sadness he felt in leaving behind a city which had never before held any attraction for him? He sighed and turned his thoughts to more important matters. Groundbreaking for the new Crimson Manor was imminent.

The jet lazily circled the city and headed east across the Atlantic. His Lordship watched as the Manhattan skyline disappeared from view, and with its disappearance, his sadness grew. He dwelt on it for a few moments and then snapped his mind shut to the wistful beckoning. He didn't have the time right now. He needed to get home.

Once at cruising altitude, Mr. Portico unstrapped himself and made his way to the bar where he mixed another drink. Two martinis, at the start of a flight, was a long-standing ritual. He walked to Lord Crimson's seat with the glass full to the brim.

"Sir?" he said.

Lord Crimson turned to Mr. Portico and started to reach for the glass. But he hesitated, not knowing why; and then, shaking his head, turned back to the window.

A personal mission of Mr. Portico's was the easing of the burden that weighed on Lord Crimson's shoulders. He was forever finding tidbits of interest wherever he could that might prove to take His Lordship's mind from whatever it was that held him so cold-bloodedly in its grip. His rate of success, so far, hadn't been impressive, but he was a persevering fellow and giving up never entered his mind.

That morning, however, he'd discovered an article in the newspaper which was so wonderfully uplifting that it appeared his dismal success rate might actually have taken a turn for the better.

"It's on page three, sir," the butler said, after taking the short walk to where His Lordship was seated. "Perhaps you'll enjoy having a look."

"Thank you," Lord Crimson said, indicating that Mr. Portico lay it down on a nearby chair.

They were half-way across the Atlantic when Lord Crimson, out of the corner of his eye, caught a glimpse of the newspaper. He felt a pang of conscience for his long-suffering butler, and if for no other reason than to make Mr. Portico feel that his efforts were not in vain, Lord Crimson picked it up. He opened it to the third page and wondered what it was that a newspaper would find of enough import that it would go to the expense of printing, on magazine quality paper, an entire page in color. He put on his glasses.

The first photo was fairly inconsequential. A teen-aged boy, watching a young girl, as she drew a picture. It was touching, and charming, but hardly worthy of such expense. There *was*, however, something oddly familiar about the boy. Perplexed, Lord Crimson shrugged his shoulders and turned his attention to the second photograph. Its caption, *Little Miss Rembrandt,* piqued his curiosity, and after adjusting his glasses, the expense became immediately apparent. A work of art, beautiful as anything he'd ever seen, had come to life at the little girl's fingertips. With a razor-sharp focus, he scrutinized the face in the portrait. She was a young noblewoman from centuries past; little more than a girl, with sparkling eyes of a deep green color he'd never seen before, and a smile that threatened to chase his sorrows away. All this from a newspaper photograph? Fascinated, he studied it further, and as he did, the beckoning returned. But now it was insistent and gave him no quarter. Lord Crimson reached for the phone.

In the cockpit, a light flashed; the pilot pressed the speaker button. "Milord?"

"If it's not too much trouble, Michael, I wish to return to New York."

Michael sighed, but he had long since learned there was no point in arguing. "Aye aye, sir," he said, and a few moments later, the plane banked, turned, and headed back toward the Big Apple.

THE DARK LORD

JANE EYRE'S INDECISIVENESS IN handling her latest and most climactic crisis ever was driving Francey crazy, and with an exasperated sigh, she tore her eyes from the book.

"Oh hi, Pop," she said. "Sorry. I didn't see you."

"Yeah," he said. "You seemed pretty involved with your friend Jane, so I didn't want to disturb you."

"No sweat. What's up?"

He sat down on her bed and took her hand. "I just wanted to see how you were doing," he said. "You know—after today."

"Well, it's funny you should ask."

"Yeah? Why's that?"

"Because I've been thinking about it. Uncle Jules and all. We had a really nice chat about art, and painters, and Rembrandt. It's actually scary how knowledgeable he is."

"Yeah," Rick said. "Lizzie says the same thing."

"So anyway, we were just talking and kidding around, when all of a sudden, he got real serious—"

An electric chill swept through Rick's body.

"—and he asked me if I knew what I was looking for. For a second, I didn't know what he meant, but then I did. I *am* looking for something, aren't I, Pop? With these dreams?"

"I don't know, babe. I sure wish I did."

"Yeah, I'm pretty sure I am. And here's the thing—I have a feeling that if I don't find it soon . . ."

Francey instantly regretted her words; and obstinate words they were; for they hung in mid-air, as if daring someone to challenge them.

Rick took her in his arms, and held her as he'd never done before. "You've got an awful lot of good people in your corner," he said. "I wouldn't worry too much about it."

"You're right, Pop," she said, with a convincing show of good cheer. "Nothing bad could ever happen to me. Not as long as you, and Alex, and Miss Gingery are around."

"I'm gonna let you get back to your reading," Rick said, and managed to disappear from her sight before she'd had a chance to see his eyes.

The phone rang. Cemented to his recliner, Rick, without budging an inch, hit the speaker button. "Yeah, Johnny, what's up?"

"Look," Johnny said, "I hate to bother you with this, and if you just say no, then that'll be it—Lord Crimson delayed his trip home. In fact, he turned the damned plane around in mid-flight. He wants to see you. In private."

"What's he want?"

"I've no idea."

What the hell was it about Lord Crimson that made him feel as if he had no choice?

"Okay," Rick said. "Where, and what time?"

After he'd hung up, Rick mused over his confounded willingness to be at Lord Crimson's beck and call. Then an idea struck him and he hit the speed-dial.

"Hello?" Lizzie said.

"Hi, it's Rick."

"Rick—what's wrong?"

"Nothing. Does something have to be wrong in order for me to call?"

"Well," she said, and he could hear her smiling, "there *has* been a precedent set."

"Yeah, okay, forget what I said."

"Done. So—what's up?"

Suddenly, he felt nervous. Heads of state; presidents of multi-billion dollar corporations; the most elite of the Hollywood elite—these people fazed him not a whit. But the thought of asking Lizzie Gingery out on a date was giving him heart palpitations. He inhaled, deep, and let it out. "How would you like to meet Lord Crimson?"

At the sound of Rick's knock, Alex shut his book and watched as Rick and Francey let themselves in.

"Have a seat, guys. She'll be out in a minute."

Francey sat down next to Alex, but Rick remained on his feet, pacing inconspicuously.

"Wow, Alex," Francey said. "You're almost done with that enormous book."

"Yeah, I'm a pretty fast reader."

"That's for sure," Rick joined in. Maybe talking would help put him at ease. "I remember reading *Bleak House* in school. It took me a whole semester just to get through it."

But before Francey had a chance to tell her father he was being silly, Lizzie breezed into the room. At the sight, both Rick's and Francey's jaws dropped.

Lizzie, in her natural state, had those rarest of good looks which needed no preparation to show them off. Simply by running a brush through her hair after jumping out of bed in the morning, and male and female heads alike would turn as she walked down the street. Tonight, however, was important. Lord Crimson would be expecting Rick to arrive alone, and she wanted to keep the disappointment to a minimum. So the correct estimation of effort for the task at hand had been taken, and the glow that surrounded her lit up the room. Rick caught himself staring and quickly averted his eyes.

"Oh, Miss Gingery," Francey said. "You're so, so beautiful."

"Sweetheart," Lizzie said. "How about, when we're not in the classroom, you call me Lizzie?"

Though she'd heard the words, Francey disbelieved her ears. Call a teacher by her first name? Such blasphemy had to have been unprecedented. She found her tongue and murmured, "Lizzie . . . Lizzie . . . Such a beautiful name."

At the loving tribute to her name, a memory appeared, and with eyes misted over, Lizzie wrapped her arms around the little girl.

When Lizzie had been of an age when children are normally fed such bedtime pap as *Jack and the Beanstalk* and *Fun With Dick and Jane*, Jonathan Gingery had, instead, spent those precious moments with his daughter reading to her from the classics: Jane Austen's *Pride and Prejudice,* for example. Every once in a while, he would look up from his reading and say, "And what beautiful creature, residing in this bed, is also named Lizzie?"

And giggling, Lizzie would say, "Oh, Daddy, stop it."

And when that night's chapter was done, Jonathan would take her in his arms and say, "My Lizzie . . . My beautiful, beautiful Lizzie."

Then, when left alone in her bed, she'd fill herself with wonder, pondering the fact that she and one of the great female characters in all of literature shared the same name. Those nights she'd spent with Jonathan and Lizzy Bennet were the stuff of dreams; and a happier child, than Lizzie Gingery, did not exist.

Dad . . .

"Listen guys," Rick said, and Lizzie's mind snapped back. "We shouldn't be too late. And we're both carrying cell phones, so—"

"Pop?"

"Yeah, babe?"

"I'm quite sure we'll be fine."

"Of course," he said. "Sorry.—Well, we'll see you guys later."

As they left the apartment, and just before the door had shut, Lizzie turned and winked at Alex.

"I saw that," Francey said, after the door had closed.

"Yeah," Alex said, grinning devilishly. "Lizzie'll probably kill me for telling you this, but . . . She really likes your dad."

"Oh Alex," Francey said, hugging herself. "Isn't this simply wonderful?"

Assisted by a valet at each door, Rick and Lizzie stepped out of the cab. The door to the private club swung open with the help of a pair of black-gloved hands, and Lizzie took a firm hold of Rick's arm. Inside, it was black as pitch.

As the door shut behind them, and the sparse light afforded by the streetlamps was left behind, Lizzie's grip tightened.

A dimly lit path showed the way to the Maitre d's podium, and before Rick had a chance to announce their arrival, the Maitre d' held up his hand signaling for silence. He studied Rick thoroughly for some moments before saying, "Mr. St. Michael?"

Rick nodded.

"Welcome to the *Dark Lord*."

"They sure got the name of this place right," Lizzie whispered. And then, turning on a flashlight to illuminate their path, the maitre d' led the way to Lord Crimson's table.

Lord Crimson stood up. He never made snap judgments, and so he would simply wait patiently to find out why his wish for this meeting to be private had gone unheeded.

"Hello, Rick," he said, as they shook hands. "It's good of you to meet me like this."

Remaining silent on that particular subject, Rick said, "Lord Crimson—this is my friend, Lizzie Gingery. Lizzie—Lord Crimson."

Lord Crimson took Lizzie's offered hand and put it to his lips. There was something wonderfully familiar in her eyes; and though he couldn't put his finger on just what it was, still it recalled to him a long forgotten tenderness, which then was stowed within his words to her.

"I had asked Rick to come alone," he said. "It was, in fact, vitally important that this meeting be solely between him and me. And yet, Lizzie Gingery—I find I am beside myself with joy that you have graced us with your presence. Now, the both of you. Please . . . sit down."

Lord Crimson's personal waiter appeared out of nowhere and silently awaited his orders.

"What's your pleasure tonight, Rick?" His Lordship asked. "Simply a glass of water . . . or a martini?"

"Let's make it a martini, sir. Straight up. Extra olives."

"And for you, my dear?"

"I'll have the same, thank you."

"My usual, Sammy," Lord Crimson said. Sammy bowed and disappeared into his inner sanctum.

"Please bear with me a few moments more," His Lordship said. "I fear I need the courage afforded me by a good stiff drink to relate what I have come here to say."

Rick seriously doubted that Lord Crimson had ever in his life needed his courage bolstered by an artificial stimulus. Probably it was more to set himself and Lizzie at ease than anything else. And if that were the case, Rick was grateful.

As they waited for their drinks, Lizzie's perceptions were hard at work. The extent to which Lord Crimson reminded her of her father was staggering. The depth of his compassion. The shrewdness of his mind. The effortlessness of his competence. But there was a difference, and it was profound. While Jonathan's eyes had sparkled with a boundless joy of life, Lord Crimson's were devoid of even the reminiscence of a glimmer. It saddened her deeply, for what she'd so quickly come to understand was, if there were ever a man who could help fill the void left in her heart by Jonathan's passing, he sat across the table from her now.

Sammy reappeared, served the drinks, and vanished.

"To Rick and Lizzie," Lord Crimson said, lifting his glass.

The toast was drunk and then Lord Crimson said, "Again Rick, thank you for coming."

Rick's nod; subtle as the movement of the stars.

"Sometimes," Lord Crimson said, his eyes on Rick, "our well thought-out priorities have no choice but to yield to that for which our hearts yearn, don't you find?"

Rick returned his stone-like gaze. He'd suspected all along where this was going and was preparing himself.

"For some years now," Lord Crimson said, "I have had a construction crew on retainer. We struck a bargain which states that whatever project they might be involved with would be dropped, immediately, upon my order. That order was issued yesterday, and though construction cannot begin without my presence, I am still here."

Lord Crimson's eyes softened as he focused them on Lizzie.

"What I'm going to say now was meant for Rick's ears alone. That I'm also willing to say it to you is nothing short of remarkable."

He took a long and thoughtful draught; and then turned back to Rick.

"This house which you have created, whose beauty for which I haven't adequate words, is more than a mere master-piece of architecture. It is a pivotal section of a puzzle which, once fully assembled, will hopefully reveal the secret of a tor-tured life. That there yet remain more pieces there is little doubt. But once it is standing, the new Crimson Manor will, I pray, cause them to fall into place. Thus I've returned for I suspect that—though it is unwitting—the piece that you your-self hold so dear, is one without which the puzzle cannot be completed. And though begging doesn't become me, if you were to tell me that it would change your mind, I'd get down on my knees. So once again I ask—how did you do it?"

It was to His Lordship's enormous credit that Rick found himself more torn by this than by anything before in his life. If only the circumstances had been otherwise, but the stakes were his daughter's life and nothing was worth the risk. Rick reflected sadly for a few moments, and shaking his head, said, "I'm sorry."

Lord Crimson accepted Rick's refusal graciously and dwelt on it no more. Another avenue to explore had opened up, for it had suddenly dawned on him what it was about Lizzie that had touched him so deeply. And with that dawning came a realization: Lizzie Gingery, unawares, held a clue to a piece of the puzzle. And he began to lay the groundwork.

"Then perhaps you would be so kind as to indulge a tired old man a few minutes more of your time. I gave my pilot a day's liberty to atone for, so inconsiderately, delaying his return to his family; and thus my journey home will have to wait. Would you mind terribly? I could use some intelligent conversation."

"Of course we don't mind . . . do we?" Lizzie said, gazing with those incredible eyes into Rick's.

"No, of course not," Rick said, minding terribly.

"So, Lizzie," Lord Crimson said. "Why don't you tell me of those fateful circumstances which brought about the convergence of your path, with Rick's?"

"Well," she said. "I teach sixth grade in the city—at the Amadeus Elementary School. Francey—Rick's daughter—is in my class."

"I see," Lord Crimson said. "Which leads me to the natural assumption that Rick must have been summoned to the school in response to a breach of proper conduct on his daughter's part. I believe this to be—at least in this day and age—the single likely circumstance in which a parent and his child's teacher would find themselves in close proximity. I must confess, though, I'm quite surprised to learn that any child of Rick's would misbehave. At least to the degree that he would be called to task for it."

Lizzie laughed. And for a moment or two, Lord Crimson's sorrows receded into the background.

"Not quite," she said. "The fact is, if Francey were any more of an angel, she'd have wings."

"And now I find myself in yet another mystery. If Francey is such a model of propriety, what could possibly have brought the two of you together?"

"Kind of a fluke, really," Lizzie said. "She got a bit too swept away by a story she was telling the class, and the result was that Rick was called in and found us together in the nurse's office."

"It must have been quite a tale."

Lizzie smiled. "Jane Austen couldn't have told a more compelling story than Francey did that day."

Lord Crimson shifted his eyes. "Your daughter would appear to be a most unusual little girl, Richard."

Richard. No one but his parents had ever called him that, and then it was only when he'd been caught with his hand in the proverbial cookie jar. Rick struggled to hide his unease. And though he noticed it, Lord Crimson forged ahead, undeterred.

"That little anecdote about Francey brings something to mind. There was an item in today's paper, which I'm quite sure you'll both find interesting. It appears that somewhere in your fair city, and apparently in utmost secrecy, another unusual little girl resides. Perhaps *unusual* isn't quite the word, for what she possesses is a gift which borders on the supernatural. Unfortunately—or fortunately—depending on your point of view, the photograph of her, although excellent, was of her back. But the young man she was with?—His picture was crystal clear. And what do you think? Why he had an uncanny resemblance to you, Elizabeth. But it was more than a simple resemblance. It was as if you shared the same soul. A wild coincidence, my dear?"

Lizzie struggled. She couldn't lie to him, yet to say anything would betray Rick's trust, and at the very least, complicate Francey's life even further. But Rick came to the rescue and interjected a comment, non-sequitur but demanding attention; and Lizzie felt as if she had just been pulled ashore after going down for the third time.

"May I say, sir," Rick said, "that your butler—Mr. Portico, isn't it?—struck me as a man who, in another life, would have had servants of his own."

Lord Crimson was actually relieved at Rick's attempt to sidetrack him, for he'd had no desire to make Lizzie uncomfortable. A reaction was all he had been after. And that having been accomplished, he addressed Rick's comment.

For some minutes, he spoke of Mr. Portico—of his seemingly endless list of sterling qualities, and of a relationship, more often than not, of two good friends, rather than master and servant. Lizzie was enchanted; but not so, Rick, for Lord Crimson's having knowledge of his daughter was the last thing he could have wanted; the weight lay like lead upon a pair of already bowed shoulders.

When what he considered a respectful amount of chit-chatting time had passed, Rick stood up and offered his hand.

"It's always a pleasure, sir," he said, with firm finality.

Lord Crimson stood up also, and said, as they shook hands, "I pray fervently, Rick, that a solution to the dilemma in which you find yourself is found quickly."

He then took Lizzie's hand and though the smile he attempted was a grim one at best, still Lizzie was aware that it had been a long, long time since another such had been bestowed. And she was touched beyond measure.

Rick and Lizzie disappeared into the darkness; His Lordship's eyes following them until the last. And had Lizzie known that her presence had reminded Lord Crimson of a time when he might, himself, have had a daughter—a time so black with tragedy that it could scarcely be imagined—she would have wept until her tears ran dry.

On their wedding day, Clara Dunnington had been twenty-three years old; and though Charlie Crimson was only a few years her senior, he was already well on his way to making his mark on the world. As much then, as now, Charlie's was a world bereft of joy. But rather than see it as an impediment to their happiness, it served only to strengthen Clara's love for him, and with a steel-like resolve, she swore that in the end it would yield to her and thenceforth be forever banished from this Earth. Charlie's brave young wife might well have succeeded, had she been given half a chance.

A year after they were wed, the Crimsons found themselves with child. Charlie, though his sadness continued unabated, now had a thread to which he could cling. Perhaps the love of a new born babe—hopefully a little girl—added to that of Clara's, would help to ease his burden.

Clara had been a delicate creature, whose slight figure bent before even the mildest of breezes. And though her soul had the strength of a thousand men, her body threatened to crumble before the task of childbirth. Taking the pregnancy to term, the doctors had said, was a risky proposition, and two months early, a caesarean section was performed. A child was taken from Clara's body—Charlie's hoped-for little girl. The infant tried valiantly, while uttering a plaintive cry, to open up her tiny eyes. But, sadly, her efforts ceased; and never even having looked upon this world, she breathed no more.

She was placed in an open casket and lay for several days while Charlie wept at her side. When he finally had the strength, he stood up, and leaning on the coffin for support, gazed at the innocent face of his dead child. The edge of his rope had been reached; his life was over. The act of ending it was all that remained.

Clara would be well provided for now that he'd achieved some financial independence. And, he also reasoned, she'd get over it in time. But now, with a clear path for a resolution to his woes having been established, Charlie was able to observe the havoc that childbirth had wrought upon Clara's fragile body. His drastic act would have to wait until she'd recovered. To desert her, in this state, was unthinkable.

But recovery for Clara was not to be, and it was a few days later that she mustered what little strength remained to her. She called his name, and Charlie took her hand.

"Promise me you'll lick this thing," she said, the quiet words as if sinking in quicksand. "It's the only way I'll be able to rest."

She paused for a moment to catch her breath and then the

last words she ever spoke fell hard upon him: "I'll be watching, Charlie, so do it for me . . . for me."

And left no choice, he promised.

Lord Crimson remained at his table in the *Dark Lord* for the few minutes more necessary to finish up his drink, and then turned his attention toward the far corner of the room. He nodded, and Mr. Portico stood up and went to fetch the car.

"Rick?"

"Yeah?" he said, looking at the floor of the cab.

"Listen, I'm sorry. I didn't see it coming."

"Don't . . . Please . . . If anyone should be apologizing, it's me. I placed you in the middle of a sordid affair that should've, in no way, involved you. It's my fault. I used the meeting as an excuse. And I'm sorry."

"An excuse?" Lizzie said. "An excuse for what?"

Sheepishly, Rick said, "I just wanted to spend some time with you."

"I see," Lizzie said. "And did you really think you needed an excuse?"

THE SHOWDOWN

"**D**ID YOU GUYS have a good time?" Francey asked, as Rick tucked her in.

"Yeah, we did."

"How'd Lizzie like him? Lord Crimson?"

"She loved him. She'd have taken him home if he'd let her."

Francey rolled her eyes. "He sounds like a pretty interesting guy."

"Yeah, he does, doesn't he?" Rick said. But having had quite enough of Lord Crimson for one night, he added, in an effort to change the subject, "So what did you guys do? You and Alex."

"Talked, mostly. He told me about what it was like, growing up with Lizzie and their dad."

"Yeah?"

"Yeah. You know what's unique about them? As a brother and sister, I mean."

"No babe, what?"

"They always got along. Alex told me that they've never fought. Not once in their entire lives."

"Wow. That *is* amazing."

"I think it's mainly because of Alex. He's so relaxed. Nothing fazes him, even in the slightest. He just takes whatever comes his way and turns it to his advantage. Just . . . easy as pie." Francey was struggling now to keep her eyes open. "You know who he reminds me of?"

"No. Who?"

"You."

"Is that so?" Rick said. "Well, I'm flattered."

"And I'm not the only one who thinks so either, you know. I mean, not that you're reminiscent of Alex, but how nothing fazes you, and you turn everything that comes along to your advantage."

"Really?" Rick said. "And who, might I ask, has been spreading tales about me out of school?"

"Johnny."

"Falstaff?"

"Yeah. Sometimes he calls me, just to chat."

"You're kidding. I had no idea."

"Yeah. He loves you, you know. Just like a son."

"I know, sweetie," Rick said, as Francey's eyelids spent their last waking flutter. "I love him too."

The year is 1670. Edward Delaney is twenty-three; Susan Sebastian—nineteen. In the clearing, under the oak tree, they are locked in an embrace. Edward tears himself away, mounts his horse, and gallops off.

Barely has Edward gone from sight when a dozen or more men, armed with swords and pistols, riding hard, enter the clearing. The leader, Lord Trumbull, approaches Lady Susan. Smirking, the slime oozing from his black soul, he says, "Where is he, Milady?"

"Go to the devil," is Lady Susan's cold, calm reply.

"By your father's oath," Lord Trumbull says, "you have been promised to me. And should Edward Delaney meet a tragic end so that I may stake my claim . . . Well, Milady, that will most assuredly be a shame."

Trumbull's smirk turns to a snarl, and kicking his horse bloody, he gallops off, his dozen men close on his heels.

Edward Delaney is no coward, but he is also no fool. Thirteen men, armed with swords and pistols, against one, armed with only a sword, are odds not exactly stacked in his favor. His horse at a dead run, Edward smiles grimly at the thought that perhaps at a later date he and Lord Trumbull will meet on a more equal footing. Thanks to his father's diligence, not only in his academic education, but also in procuring the aid of the finest fencing masters in the land, Edward's sword-fighting skills are, indeed, formidable.

Not too far distant, and straight ahead, is the forest in which Edward spent his childhood—the playground in which he caroused as a child—where every tree and bush is known better by him than any other living soul. If he can but beat his pursuers there, even by mere seconds, the forest will swallow him up as if he never existed. He draws his sword and mercilessly whips his horse to get every last ounce of speed from the beast.

Now there is the sound of gunshots, and though the accuracy of the primitive weapons is laughable, still there is the possibility of a stray bullet finding its mark—and Edward speaks to his horse. The urgency cuts through to the animal's heart, and miraculously, the noble steed's stride lengthens. Lord Trumbull and his men are no longer gaining ground.

Edward is now but scant seconds from safety and about to breathe a sigh of relief, when that one shot in a thousand tears through his horse's midsection, settling itself in the center of the animal's brave heart. As the horse goes down, Edward leaps from its back and hits the ground, somersaulting to a stop. Unhurt, dead calm, he waits as Lord Trumbull and his men slow their horses to a walk.

"Edward Delaney," Lord Trumbull announces in a grandiose manner, "you have overstepped your bounds for the last time."

"What a brave man you are, Trumbull," Edward says. "Your threats would ring hollow were you not surrounded by these swine."

"Back off, swine," Trumbull orders. "I'll need no help in dispatching this miserable vagrant." A boldness spoken with the knowledge that, should help be needed, his hired thugs have been well paid to watch his back.

He dismounts and swords are drawn. Edward peers down his blade into Trumbull's evil soul. But for the ruthless audience, the scoundrel would have been in serious trouble.

"En garde," Trumbull says, and the positions are assumed.

Trumbull attacks, and Edward puts his knowledge and skills to their first real test; never before has he been required to use his sword for anything but friendly sport. But he has learned his lessons well, and his teachers were done proud that day. Easily able to parry any and all of Lord Trumbull's offensive moves, Edward bides his time, fencing defensively, while studying his opponents strengths and weaknesses. Trumbull mistakes Edward's defensive swordplay as an inability to mount an attack—his growing confidence, evident from the sneer on his face. Observing Trumbull's smug look, Edward smiles to himself. Though he may yet die today, it won't be Lord Trumbull's sword that delivers the fatal blow.

Edward's understanding of Trumbull's skill has become sufficient; purposely, he lets down his guard. Trumbull seizes this apparent opportunity and goes for the kill. An instant later, the villain's sword is torn from his grasp, and he watches, helplessly, as it lands fifty feet from where he is standing.

The point of Edward's sword is now at Trumbull's throat, pressing forward without mercy. Tripping over his feet while forced backwards, Lord Trumbull quickly finds himself, his back against a tree. From a wound, deep, though not quite at his jugular, the warmth of his flowing blood leaves him stricken with terror; unable to utter a sound. Trumbull's eyes beg for mercy as he wonders why his hired killers don't fall on Edward, slashing him to ribbons. His band of cutthroats, however, are enjoying the show far too much to put an end to it. And Edward's dazzling swordplay has rendered them respectful; further contemplation of a cold-blooded murder is now unthinkable.

Good fortune, today, smiles on Lord Trumbull, for Edward Delaney is no killer. A lesson learned at the hands of a more skillful swordsman should suffice, the lad reasons, and backing off slightly, he says, "If Lord Sebastian could see you now, he would, no doubt, rethink his choice for the husband of his daughter."

"Perhaps," Trumbull says, unsteadily, "but it matters little, for as you can see, Lord Sebastian is nowhere to be found."

With the realization that Edward has no intention of ending his life, Trumbull's boldness returns. "Showing your face again, Mr. Delaney, would not be a wise decision on your part. But in the spirit of good sportsmanship, I give you fair warning. If you do not heed my words, I will not answer for the consequences."

"I will leave for now," Edward says, "but our paths will cross again, for it is Susan's decision as to whom she is wed."

Edward turns toward the safety of his forest, for Trumbull has spoken the oath of 'good sportsmanship' and would no longer dare to shoot a man in the back.

But the youth has been too lenient with his credit; with Edward now safely out of striking range, Trumbull draws his pistol, takes careful aim, and fires. The bullet lodges in Edward's heart, and Lady Susan's young lover is dead before he hits the ground. Trumbull walks to the limp body, which lies still upon the grass. "Alas, my unfortunate friend . . . Not anymore."

Alex woke, and as he sat bolt upright, the perspiration pouring down his face, and the sound of his heartbeat pounding on his eardrums, all he could feel was the bullet tearing through Edward Delaney's back, stilling our young hero's heart forever.

MR. PORTICO

"**P**OP, YOU DIDN'T wake me," Francey said, as she came bounding into the kitchen. "You didn't think I was staying home from school again, did you?"

Rick looked up from his second cup of coffee that morning. "Relax, kiddo. Lizzie knows you're going to be late. I'll just drop you on my way to the office."

"Whew," she said, and sat down.

Rick had set out a bowl of cereal for her, and she poured some milk into it. After chewing thoughtfully for a minute, she set her spoon down. "I'm curious about something," she said.

"Yeah? What's that?"

"Is Lord Crimson some kind of royalty? Being a lord and all?"

"No. He earned it—his title."

"Whoa. Heavy. So what did he do, exactly, to earn it?"

"Well . . . I don't know, *exactly*, what he did, but I do know approximately."

"*Pop.*"

"Okay, approximately then," he said, chuckling. "From what I've gathered, his acts of kindness and charity over the years have touched more lives than can be counted. He's as selfless—do you know what that means? Selfless?"

"Of course, Pop. I'm not a child, you know."

"Right. Sorry. Anyway, he's apparently as selfless a person as you could ever imagine."

"Really?" she said. "You know, I think maybe I'd like to meet him."

"Well, anything's possible. But you *do* realize that he lives in England, right? And once his new home is built, I doubt very much that he'll be straying far."

"Why?"

"It's complicated."

"Pop."

"All right, all right," Rick said, and then he told her about eternal searches, and tortured souls, and of puzzles that may or may not be solved by the building of a house.

"That's so sad," she said. "But it just makes me want to meet him all the more—"

All the more, Rick mused to himself.

"—because I bet I could help him conquer it—his sadness and stuff."

"You know what, sweetie? I think that if anyone could help him, it would be you. And now that you've got me thinking about it, remember I told you that I was going to take some time off after this last project? Well, it seems to me that a drastic change of scenery would do us both an awful lot of good, so . . . maybe I'll arrange for us to take a trip abroad."

"Oh Pop, really? Really and truly?"

"Yeah, babe. Really and truly."

Rick had barely sat down, when Bea, beaming like a proud parent, marched in.

"You're quite the hero, you know," she announced.

"Yeah, yeah, I know."

"In case you're interested," she said, handing Rick his coffee, *"Architectural Digest* is coming over to do a huge spread on you and Crimson Manor."

Exasperated, Rick sighed.

"You know, Rick," Bea said, "most people would be, at least, somewhat happy about something like this."

"Yeah? Well, I'm not most people, now am I?"

"Boy, that's for damn sure," she said, and with a shake of her head, left Rick to himself.

The Falstaff Architectural Firm was as busy as it had ever been. Too many projects with impossible deadlines, and way too few hours in the day. If anything, the fact that he'd get no argument from Johnny made Rick feel even worse about taking time off.

Johnny was on the phone. He motioned for Rick to take a seat and voiced a polite excuse to whomever he was speaking.

"Hi," Johnny said.

"Hi." Rick said, and he took a breath. "Listen, Johnny—"

"No, Rick—you listen. I've never interfered in your life without an invitation, and I'm not about to start, but I suspect that whatever's going on with you and Francey is more significant than anything I've been able to come up with. My only request is that you help Matthews and Josephson with some of the specs on the new Atlanta museum, and then I want you out of here. And I don't want to see your face anywhere in this vicinity until whatever it is that's sending your life into such bedlam is handled. And I'm not kidding around here."

Rick never felt so much like hugging anyone in his life, but he restrained himself and said, simply, "Thanks, Johnny. I'll go see to the museum for you."

Rick turned to leave, and as he reached the door, Johnny called his name. Rick turned to him.

"Whatever it is that's going on," Johnny said, with moisture in his eyes, "if you need anything . . . anything at all . . ."

The way Johnny Falstaff lived his life defined so many things for so many people. For Rick, though, it was his uncompromising friendship that was the most defining thing of all.

It was five o'clock, and, as usual, Francey stepped off the school bus in front of her brownstone. As she approached the stairway to the building, she noticed a man, his back straight as an arrow, sitting on the stoop. He was immaculately dressed, from the mirror shine on his shoes to the dapper derby atop his head, and as she drew near, he stood up and removed his hat.

"Have I the pleasure of addressing Miss Francey St. Michael?" he said, with a very proper British accent.

She studied him for a moment, and ascertained that it was unlikely that this pleasant, well-mannered gentleman posed any threat.

"Yes," she said.

"My name is Mr. Portico, and if you will allow it, I'd appreciate a word with you."

"Well . . . Perhaps I'll allow it," she said.

Mr. Portico chuckled. "You, my dear, are a wise and charming young lady."

"Thank you."

"Do you, perchance, know who Lord Crimson is?"

"Of course." Francey said. "He's Pop's client."

First, Rick St. Michael, and now this disconcertingly charming little girl of his. My lord, what a dramatic shift there'd been, in just these last few days, with respect to Mr. Portico's view of Americans.

"Yes. Precisely right," he said. "I am a friend of Lord Crimson's and am here at his request. To deliver a message to you. Actually, to ask a favor of you."

"Me? Really? No kidding?"

"Yes, my dear, no kidding. You see, His Lordship has found himself in a bit of a dilemma. He can't seem to find the location upon which his new home should be built. He was wondering if, perhaps, you could assist him?"

"Would you like a cup of coffee?" she said.

"Thank you, Miss Francey, but I don't wish to intrude."

Francey smiled. She was starting to like this guy and his accent was so delightful.

"First of all," she said, "it's not an intrusion. And second of all, we have to go upstairs anyway in order to find the location."

Still hesitant, Mr. Portico said, "I'm not sure how happy your father would be—"

"Oh, don't worry about Pop. He's stuck at the office."

"You're quite certain?"

"Yes. Quite. I just spoke to him a couple of minutes ago, and he's gotta explain a bunch of stuff to some of the other guys at work. It'll be hours before he gets home."

Mr. Portico conceded, and they went upstairs.

A short while later, Francey handed Mr. Portico a freshly brewed cup of coffee made from Rick's secret stash: a blend he had imported, regularly, on the black market, straight from Paris; a blend which those wonderfully sophisticated Parisians purposely tried to keep out of the hands of those insipid American low-lifes who wouldn't know a good cup of coffee from a weak cup of tar.

"Thank you, Miss Francey," the butler said, and after taking a few dainty sips, he added, "This is quite delicious . . . for coffee."

"You're welcome," she said. Francey took great pride in her coffee-making skills. "I've already had my caffeine allotment for the week, or I'd join you."

Subtly, Francey watched Mr. Portico as he sipped his coffee. He certainly had good table manners.

"Have you and Lord Crimson been friends long?" she inquired.

"Yes, quite a long time, actually." He thought for a moment. "It will be thirty five years, this coming September."

"Yes, that *is* quite a long time, isn't it?" she said. "Pop says he's a pretty important guy."

Mr. Portico found Rick's understatement amusing, and said, "I daresay, Miss Francey, if you but knew the extent to which—" He stopped himself; it was best to leave those details well enough alone. And said, instead, "Lord Crimson is one of the most well-respected men in England."

"You must be pretty important too," Francey said, "to be such good friends with him."

The butler paused to formulate a reply. His importance couldn't be denied, but it was of a very personal nature. "I indulge myself in thinking that I *am* important . . . at least, to His Lordship."

"Well," Francey said, "from where I'm sitting, I'd say that was a foregone conclusion."

Mr. Portico averted his eyes; best they should get to the business at hand.

"I assume Lord Crimson is anxious for this information," Francey said, sensing the butler's thoughts, "so why don't we see if I can't figure out where his new home should be built?" And she led the way out of the kitchen.

"I'm pretty sure there's an old book of maps here some-where," she said, as she walked toward the bookcase in the living room.

"I brought a map," Mr. Portico said, and Francey turned to see him removing a folded-up map from his breast pocket.

"Oh good," she said, and together they spread it out on the conference table. Mr. Portico stepped back in order to give her plenty of room, and watched, fascinated, as she, while making thoughtful sounds, studied the layout of the land. She opened the drawer and removed a yellow magic marker.

"May I?" she said.

"The map is yours. Do with it as you will."

Francey made a small circle and then beckoned to Mr. Portico. "This is where the house should be," she said. "But there's no way you could find it just from the map, so I'm thinking that what's needed here is a picture. You know—something that shows the surrounding countryside."

Mr. Portico agreed, while wondering from whence this picture would arrive.

"I should warn you," Francey said, "that to get this exactly right, it might take a little while, so maybe you should get comfortable. Pop loves his recliner; I think he'd live in it if he could, so if you want . . ."

Mr. Portico politely declined her offer. Whatever was about to happen, he wanted a ringside seat, and as Francey, in readiness, set down pastels and sketchpad, he asked, "Do you mind, very much, if I stand here?"

"Not even the tiniest bit," was her reply.

Mr. Portico was by no means an uneducated man, and in the arts, was actually quite sophisticated. But even so, he couldn't remember when last he'd seen anything as beautiful as the English countryside which flowed from Francey's fingers onto the paper beneath them. He stilled his breathing, and quieted the beating of his heart. And stood, transfixed, 'til she was done.

Francey sat for a minute after setting down her pastels, and studied the two illustrations she had made. Satisfied, she turned to Mr. Portico. "Okay," she said, pointing to one of the drawings. "If you're standing in the middle of the property, this is the view to the north. And this other one is the view to the south. I think that should handle Lord Crimson's dilemma, don't you?"

Finally Mr. Portico had come to understand that this was not the first time he had seen this miraculous child. She was, of course, the little girl in the newspaper article that he had saved for Lord Crimson. And with the startling realization that it was he who had fastened the connection between Francey and Lord Crimson, Mr. Portico's eyes, for the first time in as long as he could remember, filled due to something other than the sorrow he felt for his master.

"Thank you, Miss Francey," he said. "And Lord Crimson thanks you as well."

"You're both very welcome," she said.

The butler walked to the front door, and as he opened it, he said, "Miss Francey, may I ask a favor?"

"Sure. Anything."

"Let's keep my visit here just between you and me. Lord

Crimson would be most unhappy if he thought he had caused your father any distress."

"Tell His Lordship not to sweat it," she said. "It'll be our little secret."

"Excellent," Mr. Portico said, as he placed his hat atop his head. "I'll relay your words to him exactly—not to sweat it. He'll find it comforting. Thank you."

He tipped his hat and closed the door behind him, leaving Francey feeling, somehow, that she had just given unto Lord Crimson, a gift upon which no price could be placed.

THE FINAL HORROR

THE WIND COMING off the river was as raw and vicious as any she could remember, and the deserted streets made her feel that in all the city, she alone was willing to brave the cold. Suddenly a solitary taxicab careened wildly around the corner. Honking at nothing in particular, it quickly disappeared from sight, leaving Lizzie, desolate, in the center of the busiest city in the world. She shoved her hands deeper into her pockets and focused on the street signs while she counted down the remaining blocks that lay ahead. Struggling to get her mind off the ferocious cold, she steered her thoughts toward the previous night's events.

That Lord Crimson had made the connection between Lizzie and Alex was not even up for debate. She was curious, though, to see what he might do with that information. Curious, but not concerned. Rick, though, had to be in a turmoil over it being too close to the situation for objectivity to reign. She'd call him when she got home—to put his mind at ease.

Rick. She so loved it that he found her a comfort. Lizzie was well aware that under normal circumstances he was quite capable of doing without help in any quarter at all, thank you. And that was all right too. Because she didn't mind being comforted herself on those rare occasions when it might be needed. Lizzie smiled to herself, thinking of Rick's arms around her during one of those exceptional times. Or anytime at all, for that matter.

With no warning, a gust of wind, nay, a thousand tiny missiles formed of ice, shot, as if from a cannon sitting on the river's surface, through Lizzie's poor, shivering body. In desperation, she searched for the next street sign. The solemn lamppost materialized from within the darkness. Two blocks to go. Lizzie gritted her teeth.

She thought of Lord Crimson's anguish, endured for a lifetime while engaged in a never-ending search for . . . what? A resolve to help him had grown, seemingly, by the minute since she and Rick had left him at the *Dark Lord*, but puzzling over how exactly that was to be accomplished would have to wait. Right now, it was just too damned cold.

Ah, she thought, the bitter irony. If only Francey could manage that—to somehow block the memory which threatened to tear the child's soul from her body. If only . . .

Lizzie's struggle for her own survival had now become almost frantic, and all other thoughts were forced to the sidelines. Her entire focus was on the entrance to her building as she rounded the final corner leading home. And the connection she had come so close to making—that of a hidden memory which sought, relentlessly, to tear apart every fiber of Lord Crimson's being—and that of a singularly horrific torment which bode so ill for Francey would, unfortunately, not be made that night.

The front door opened. When Lizzie didn't show herself in the kitchen, Alex went to seek her out. She was in the living room sitting on a towel draped over the radiator.

"Pretty brutal out, huh?" he said, while briskly rubbing her arms and back.

Her reply was a convulsive shudder that shook her entire

body. Alex continued the warmth-giving massage until life finally returned to her flesh.

"Coffee?" she said, hopefully.

"There's a fresh pot on the stove."

A few good steaming draughts of coffee later and Lizzie was able to observe that something was amiss. Alex was unusually quiet; even somber. Then she remembered that he had still been in bed when she'd left for work that morning. Also unusual. She waited to hear what was going on. And a moment later—

"Remember you told me that Uncle Jules said that Francey was looking for something—or someone—and that it was critical for us to find it soon?"

Lizzie felt the spectre of skeletal-like fingers tightening around her windpipe; and in a steady voice, masking frightening undertones, Alex said, "I know what she's looking for."

As if bolted to the chair, Lizzie listened as Alex, in chilling, graphic detail, related the events leading up to the cold-blooded murder of Edward Delaney. And though Edward's body now lay buried deep beneath the ground, his *essence*, spoken of by Uncle Jules, yet remained above; and as real to Alex now, as it had been to Edward then, the boy went on from where the dream left off.

"Of course Trumbull lied to Lord Sebastian about how Edward was killed, giving him some cock and bull story about duels of honor and other such garbage. And even though Susan knew how good Edward was with a sword and that there was no way Trumbull could have beaten him, she was too grief-stricken to make any kind of a big deal out of it; and since autopsies, at the time, were frowned upon by the church, the real cause of Edward's death went to his grave with him. After the burial, Susan proceeded to lock herself away from the world; and then, refusing to speak, eat, or sleep; she just withered herself away.

Alex took a moment to gather himself; the memory was strong.

"Anyway," he said, "this is the important part. Susan was close to death and her father was at her side, desperately trying to reconcile with her. And she cursed him—told him to rot in hell. With her dying breath, she damned him forever."

"Sounds like he deserved it," Lizzie said.

"Yeah, it does, doesn't it?—But the truth is, Lord Sebastian had no idea what Trumbull was up to. And if he *had* known, he'd have made sure the bastard was hung for his crime. He was actually a decent guy—albeit mired in the class restrictions of his time."

"Sweetheart, I don't understand," Lizzie said. "What are you saying, exactly?"

"I'm saying that Susan—Francey—needs to find her father. She needs to find him and forgive him before . . ."

Alex prepared himself for what was to follow, and Lizzie, with fists clenched, and fingernails dug deep into the palms of her hands, felt no pain, and saw no blood. But she was able to hear, and what she heard she wouldn't soon forget.

"Another one's coming," Alex said, "and this one's going to make the others seem like a walk in the park. And if I can't bring her out of it, it'll kill her."

Among Lizzie's more amazing attributes was her ability to remain strong when men of stone were crumbling all around her. Much like Scarlett O'Hara in *Gone With The Wind*, Lizzie would square her shoulders during times of adversity, and her nerves would become like steel. Unbreakable, unbendable steel. But unlike Scarlett, who would put it off until another day, Lizzie would, looking it square in the teeth, grasp it by the throat and squeeze the life from it until it lay dead at her feet.

Fifteen years earlier, when her mother had lain fatally ill and the end was drawing near, Lizzie's inflexible strength made its first appearance. For weeks she had stood by, helplessly, watching her father's will to live fade, and it became clear to her that if nothing were done, his life, and her mother's, would end together. She went to sleep one night vowing with all her might to prevent it from happening. The following morning, Lizzie awoke to find that her mother had passed away, peacefully, during the night. And that strength and courage both now filled her soul to overflowing.

Lizzie was unyielding in her doggedness to help her father overcome his grief. Not for an instant did she grieve in his presence, but reserved those times for late at night, alone in her room, with only her memories for company. Never was she less than loving, understanding, comforting—and always encouraging and upbeat. Until his dying day, Jonathan would remember his little girl, just barely thirteen years old at the time, holding his hand and saying, "It's okay, Dad, I'm going to get you through this. And don't even think about arguing, because you don't have a choice."

And he would recall how her eyes, when she spoke to him thus, were always dry and full of cheer and high hopes for the future.

It had been a heroic deed of courage and strength, lo those fifteen years ago, but it would be as nothing when compared with what awaited her that night.

Francey sat on her bed, the covers over her legs, her back against the headboard. Alex sat on the edge, close by. She was well aware of what that night likely held in store for her. No one had mentioned a word. But she knew.

"Alex?" she said, in a voice so soft and sweet.

He smiled. "Yeah, Francey. I'm here."

"You know what's really too bad?"

He made no reply, knowing that whatever she was going to say would leave his heart broken, with little chance of its ever mending.

"What's really too bad is that now that we've finally found each other, it looks like, once again, we're going to have to wait. It's all pretty frustrating, don't you think?"

His throat tightened; he concentrated on holding back his tears.

"You remember now, don't you?" she said. "I mean everything, right? Every last little thing?"

He nodded.

"I knew you would. You just needed a little help—to jog your memory." Francey smiled comfortingly. "I poured my whole heart and soul into that portrait. I knew if I could bring Susan back to life, that she'd remind you of the love we had, and you'd have no choice but to remember."

Francey lowered her head and smoothed the covers. As she did, a teardrop splashed down upon the blanket. She touched it, spreading it around for a moment or two, and then she raised her brimming eyes to Alex's, and his heart was torn from his chest.

"I know it's silly to say this," she said, "but I'll try to convince you anyway. Later, in the weeks and months to come, when you think of me and you feel sad, just remember that I haven't gone away forever. I'll be back, and I'll find you . . . or you'll find me. And sooner or later, we'll be together. And if you can just really, really remember that, maybe you won't be quite so sad. Okay? . . . Alex?"

Alex nodded, forcing a smile, faint though it was. And then, for a little while, they spoke of other things. Happier things. Happier times.

In the tomblike atmosphere of Rick's kitchen, a full pot of coffee sat untouched on the stove.

"I spoke to Uncle Jules," Lizzie said. "He's making calls to everyone he can think of who's been of help to him in his research."

Rick, blankly, looked up at her. "Good. That's good."

"For the first time that I can remember," Lizzie said, "I've been praying. If there's a God, there's no way He'll allow any harm to come to Francey. There's just no way . . ."

Lizzie felt herself giving in to feelings of despair, and silently she called out for her reserve of strength. It surged within her, strong and tireless; tonight, no matter what lay ahead, she would prevail; no force on Earth had strength enough to bend those bands of steel which ran along her spine.

Rick glanced at the clock. It was getting late. "I'm gonna go check on the kids," he said, and left Lizzie staring into an empty coffee cup.

He came quietly into the bedroom where Alex and Francey, their heads close together, were talking in hushed tones. At Rick's appearance, they turned toward him.

"Hi Pop," Francey said, softly as a ray of sun, bouncing off the morning dew.

Alex stood up. "I'll just leave you two alone."

Rick sat down on Francey's bed and pushed her hair back, smoothing it gently, the way he always did when putting her to bed. "How're you doing, sweetheart?"

The thought of dying didn't frighten, so much as sadden her. She was having such a wonderful life; and now, with Alex and Lizzie firmly a part of it, the thought of leaving it behind lay heavy upon the child's heart.

"Not so good," she answered, and for the first time in his life, Rick saw sadness in his daughter's eyes.

"We're all here, sweetheart. Lizzie, and Alex, and me. And we'll be watching out for you. So don't worry. Okay?"

"I'll try. But it's hard. This feeling I have, it's telling me—" She paused to swallow a sob. "It's telling me that this time I won't be coming back."

Rick's courage reached heretofore uncharted heights as he said, almost cheerfully, "Don't be silly. Of course you're coming back. And we'll all laugh about this in the morning."

He spent a few more moments, tucking in her blankets, and smoothing her hair just a little bit more. Then he kissed her forehead.

"Good night, sweetheart. I'll come back and check on you in a little while."

"Good-bye, Pop," she said. "Good-bye." The second time a whisper.

Somehow Rick made it to the sofa. In a sorrow-filled, dream-like world, he felt Lizzie take his hand and put it to her lips. He hoped she would say something. She must know what a comfort her voice was to him.

"Rick?" she said, answering his thoughts.

Was it possible a sound could be so full of love and understanding? In the surreal setting, Lizzie appeared as an angel of mercy, there to see him through the night. He listened; she always gave him hope.

"Don't ask me how I know this," she said, "but somehow, it's all going to resolve. The answer is staring us in the face. All we have to do is see it."

Rick nodded, trying to believe.

"In her whole life," he said, "she's never known so much as one tiny drop of sadness. But when she said good-bye to me—"

A single, violent sob wracked his body. And when the aftershocks had settled down, he saw her eyes were just a blur; so with her fingertips she dried his tears. And silently they waited.

One hour later, a voice sent a ripple through the silent air. "She's asleep," Alex said. "I couldn't keep her up any longer. I'm sorry."

Rick took his eyes off the floor. "It's all right, Alex. I didn't expect you to keep her awake forever."

Vigilantly, Rick sat by her bed. Three hours had passed peacefully by, but there were yet too many that remained. Then, as if to let him know that hope tonight was, at best, a straw ungrasped, there came a movement, slight, but real. Rick brought his breathing to a standstill and tried to will the dream away. Francey's barely noticeable fidgeting stopped for a moment—just long enough for him to think about breathing again—and then his heart sank for good. The nightmare had returned; and with a vengeance.

The effort would be in vain, but still he had to try. "Francey, sweetheart. Wake up," he begged. But she was in a distant land too far away to hear.

Rick picked her up, the tears pouring forth from beneath her butterfly-like eyelids, and he carried her into the living room, where Alex had been asleep on the sofa, and Lizzie in his recliner. But they were awake now. Waiting.

Alex took Francey from Rick's arms and held her for a moment, hoping their closeness would be enough. But he was hoping against hope, as were they all, and they watched as Francey opened her eyes. There was terror in them, but a tenderness in her voice and in her touch as she held Alex's head gently in her hands.

"Edward, oh dear God. Edward."

"Francey, it's okay," Alex said. "I'm okay. Look at me, see? I'm fine."

She opened her eyes wider, and looking right through him, made a sound so terrifying—so blood-curdling—it was as if it had originated from another world. A world where terror was the norm.

Alex held her tighter—spoke louder. "Francey—Susan— I'm here. I'm right here. Please, please, just look at me."

Again, she looked through him, and her hysteria reached a height such that should it remain so for only a short while longer, it would snuff the life from her as if she were nothing better than a burnt-out candle.

All Francey could see were those first few moments when, as Susan Sebastian, she had cast her eyes, blinded by the sunlight, upon Edward's dead body. As real now, as it had been then, her face was in the dirt and her fingers were bloodied from clawing at the earth beneath the horse's hooves. Held in its stranglehold, reliving the horror over and over again, she grew weaker, while the dream grew stronger. And not until it had achieved its final victory would the nightmare relinquish its hold.

Still the ferocity of the dream continued to grow. No longer able to catch her breath, the gasps of a little girl choking on her own sobs filled the room with a stark, grim terror. Alex surrendered to his helplessness. He fell to his knees, sobbing—the child draped across his legs.

Now it was Lizzie's turn. With Francey clutched in her arms, she spoke gently, quietly, lovingly, while in her mind she sought to destroy the dream. To no avail. Lizzie redoubled her efforts: she coaxed, she pleaded, she commanded. Still nothing, and though she remained strong, a doubt had begun creeping into her consciousness. The answer, which she had been so certain was staring them in the face, had failed to show itself, and her promise to Rick—her oath that the horror would, in the end, come to naught—would be broken, leaving in its wake a tragedy too unspeakable to contemplate. In her place, another would long since have perished with hopelessness.

And that's when it happened. Rick, in his hysteria, started across the room, his intention: 911. But he stopped dead in his tracks; the sudden ringing of the telephone having crippled what was left of his sensibilities.

To Lizzie, however, in all of creation, no lilting musical phrase had ever sounded so beautiful; and with the speed of a diving falcon, she grabbed up the phone.

"Who is this?" she shouted.

"Lizzie, it's Lord Crimson."

Stunned, she stammered, "What?—How?—"

"Put the phone to Francey's ear," he said.

"But—"

"Dear God, Lizzie. Just do it!"

At which, she obeyed.

In disbelief, Rick drew close, and Alex, still on his knees, unburied his head from his hands. Was it their imaginings, or was Francey's torture losing some of its soul-shattering intensity? With hearts beating on kettle drums, they waited, and the only miracle that any of them would ever truly care about again was born before their eyes. The screams had softened; the sobs were dying out; and in only a few moments more, the little girl had arrived back home.

"Pop," she said, struggling with the weight of her arms as she held them out to him.

Lizzie gave his daughter over to him, and Francey—weak, exhausted, and spent—wrapped her arms around her father's neck, and while he wept, she comforted him.

No longer needed, Lizzie let go her implacable strength. And with tears cascading from her eyes, she sobbed into the telephone. "She's all right now. She's all right. But how? . . . How?"

"Hush, my child," Lord Crimson said. "It's gone now. Gone forever. Hush. Hush."

Only from a place where angels congregate could such a voice have come; and a new-born father had truly been given unto Lizzie Gingery that day.

"At four o'clock this afternoon," she heard him say through her tears, "my car will come for the four of you. It will take you to my private aircraft which will, in turn, ferry you across the pond. There will be a car to meet you in London which will bring you all to me. And don't bother packing. Whatever your needs, they will be provided."

"But—"

"No buts. All four of you."

"Okay," she murmured. "Okay . . ."

Numb, Lizzie hung up the phone. From the sofa, Rick, Francey, and Alex stared at her, wondering who the person on the phone could have been. The miracle worker who had saved Francey's life. Lizzie's eyes scanned her anxiously awaiting audience and they came to rest on Rick.

"That was Lord Crimson," she said. "It looks like we're taking a trip."

CONCLUSION

O UTSIDE THE INTERNATIONAL Terminal at London's Heathrow Airport, Mr. Portico stood, waiting. His jaw was clenched; his backbone, straight; and the onslaught of emotions threatening to surface would certainly find no willing participant in Mr. Portico today. Then, through the glass-paneled entrance, he saw her approach. The door opened; her eyes grew wide as saucers; and with a joyous shriek, Francey flew into the butler's arms.

"Oh, Mr. Portico," she cried, her voice so full of love and life and joy and happiness. "It's so, so wonderful to see you again."

Poor Mr. Portico didn't stand a chance, and with Francey clutched in his arms, he wept with joy. The butler's overflowing eyes found Francey's bewildered father, and he said, "All explanations will be made by Lord Crimson, sir. Now if you please . . ." And after he and Francey had unwound from each other's arms, he led them to Lord Crimson's Rolls-Royce limousine.

As Mr. Portico slid into the driver's seat, he found Francey comfortably settled in the passenger seat at his side.

"Miss Francey," he said, "Wouldn't you find it more suitable in the back? With your family?"

Francey put her arm through his, and lay her head on his shoulder. "You're my family too, Mr. Portico," she said. "Didn't you know?"

After an hour's drive—give or take—the butler pulled the car to the side of the road. And once his precious cargo had been released, Mr. Portico stood proudly by, while the majestic English Countryside swept them all away.

They were afloat upon a sea of peaceful colors; and above, seemingly close enough to touch, billowy white clouds were painted liberally onto an unearthly sky blue canvas. A short distance off stood a forest so thick with trees it was as if you could stroll along the treetops, while leisurely searching for the pot of gold at the end of the rainbow. And surrounding them, as far as they could see, the rolling hills and meadows, shimmering in the sunlight, gave them visions of Susan Sebastian and Edward Delaney bidding them welcome to their enchanted land.

After a few moments, Mr. Portico broke in quietly. "He's at the bottom of the hill," and with his eyes he showed them where to look. Down an incline, a few hundred feet away, were the remains of an old stately manor. Scattered about were all manner of construction machines, and on an ancient stone wall sat the figure of a man.

"Please . . . Go to him," the butler said. "You see, he's been waiting for you."

They started down the hill, and nearby, a tall, proud oak tree made its presence known.

"Pop, look," Francey gasped. "My tree. My wonderful, wonderful tree."

They turned, and there it was. The storybook oak tree which had no doubt been standing for hundreds of years, back even when the young noblewoman had spent so many blissful hours among its branches, stood there still, patiently awaiting the return of the young mistress of Sebastian Manor.

"It's the same. It's all exactly the same. Oh Pop, isn't it just so beautiful?"

Rick squeezed her hand to let her know that every bit as much as she, so he felt it too. Then they continued down the hill and as they approached, the man sitting on the wall stood and slowly turned to face them. His eyes sought and came to rest on Francey, and she returned his gaze. Her heart was torn, for she had known and loved him well, a long, long time ago. But as of yet she knew not how. Nor as of yet she knew from where. She rode upon her thoughts as they flew back in time until they'd come to rest upon an old familiar face. And in just another moment, it all fell into place.

"Papa?" she whispered.

His tears gathered quickly; his lips began to quiver.

"Papa," she screamed, and flung herself into his arms. And as Lord Crimson clung in desperation to his daughter from the distant past, she spoke the words he'd waited forever to hear. "Oh, Papa—I forgive you. I forgive you."

And together they wept as neither one had ever wept before.

The search was over. The nightmare, destroyed.

That evening, after dinner, Francey and Alex were heavily engaged in conversation with Mr. Portico, leaving Rick and Lizzie alone with Lord Crimson. They sat in the main study— Rick and His Lordship, smoking a couple of Cuban cigars, and all were enjoying snifters of the finest brandy in Lord Crimson's possession.

"So finally," Lord Crimson was saying, "after all these years of searching, your house—my house—Lord Sebastian's house—started awakening the dormant memories within me, attempting to unlock the secret as to why I've been so tortured by something long forgotten. When I saw the picture of Alex in the newspaper, there was something about him that I recognized. He was part of the puzzle, but where he fit, I knew not. Then, when you so defiantly brought this beautiful angel to our meeting—for which I forgave you the instant I set my eyes upon hers—that piece dropped neatly into place. Lizzie and the boy in the photograph were unquestionably brother and sister. Which meant that *Little Miss Rembrandt* had to be your daughter, Rick. As surely as she was the little girl of whom Lizzie spoke so fondly."

"I still don't understand," Rick said, "what made you think that Francey could have had anything to do with Sebastian Manor, let alone know where it used to stand."

"Ah," Lord Crimson said. "I wish I could take credit for a brilliant piece of detective work, but the fact is, it came to me in a dream. You see, that night—during a recurring nightmare that has plagued me since time immemorial—I was finally, and for the first time, able to recall at least some little bits and pieces of the dream. And who do you suppose appeared there in a starring role? Why it was none other than *Little Miss Rembrandt's* beautiful young noblewoman. She stood outside an ancient manor exactly like the one most recently conceived; and with a smile and arms outstretched, she beckoned for me to come home. The next morning, with my suspicions thus alerted, I asked Mr. Portico to perform a bit of undercover work, the result of which was—well, need I say more?"

Lord Crimson paused, his eyes, twinkling. "My poor, long-suffering butler. I believe he hasn't yet recovered from an unsavory business that went well beyond his job description. And I do ask your pardon for that trick we played on you, but it turns out it was for the best, wouldn't you agree?"

"And what about the phone call," Rick said, "right when—I mean, how could you possibly have known?"

"Again I beg your forgiveness. None of you has been out of my sight since our rendezvous at *The Dark Lord*. Indeed, a veritable army has been camped in close proximity to both your front doors ever since. At the sound of Francey's cries, I was immediately contacted, and what I felt upon hearing her anguish rent my body nearly in two. In despair I listened closely, somehow knowing that within the dream lay the answer which we both so desperately sought. Then I heard it—her lover's name cried out in agony, whereupon my remorse increased beyond all imaginings; and when it approached the limits of a man's capacity to withstand pain, suddenly, and as if by magic, the wall which had forever blocked my memory simply crumbled into dust, clearing the way for me to see the pieces of the puzzle dropping neatly into place. And with its solution, one critical thing became clear—only the sound of my voice could loosen the nightmare's stranglehold."

"If I had confided in you," Rick quietly admitted, more to himself than to Lord Crimson, "you could've ended this early on,".

"Yes, that's probably true."

"You begged me."

"Yes, Rick, but you can't blame yourself. You were protecting your precious daughter. How could you have known? How could you possibly have known?"

Rick lowered his eyes, unable to reply.

"A slight change of subject," His Lordship said, "if no one objects." Lizzie smiled, and nodded, for Lord Crimson's communication was directed toward her.

"Perhaps, my beautiful Elizabeth, you are already aware

of this, but if not, then let me be the one who enlightens you. There can, of course, be no argument that Francey is the most astounding phenomenon to find her way to the surface of this planet in quite some time. And yet, she is not alone. There is another who also possesses that same, unexplainable quality which places certain beings on a plateau high above us mere mortals. He is someone with whom I believe you are well acquainted. His name is Rick St. Michael."

As used to high praise as Rick had become, still he found it difficult to hear these words from the lips of the man whose approval he had sought so passionately. And left no choice, he looked away.

"How my heart ached with every new creation Rick submitted, for never have I seen the like. Mr. Portico, without a doubt the toughest critic known to man, described Rick's work as, not merely better, but on an altogether different plane of existence from anything heretofore submitted. And, should we dare proceed even further into the realm of the supernatural, we find that here was a man whose perceptions were such that, as incomprehensible as the concept would surely have been to anyone else, he was able to understand that I was searching for something—something for which the house was key—and proceeded to take on that search himself. It gave me hope and comfort both, knowing that there existed someone who had joined me in my mission. And even had he known the astronomical odds stacked against him, still I suspect he'd never have given up."

Lord Crimson, reflecting, drank from his glass and drew deeply on his cigar.

"I finally realized what it was that was missing. And had you searched a thousand years, still you would not have found it. Would you like to hear?"

It was to a pair of stone figures that Lord Crimson revealed the answer.

"Every day, when the original manor was being built, and even long afterwards, Susan would sit for hours perched among the topmost branches of her tree. From there, as if she were an angel looking down from Heaven, a glow sprang forth, touching indelibly all within its reach. She was the breath; the beating heart; the life itself; without which Sebastian Manor would have been forever but an empty shell. In other words, and what I'm so feebly trying to say, is that the missing element was our wondrous little noblewoman herself. You see, to guide the spirit of Sebastian Manor home, it was Francey's hand that had to hold the pen."

With a handkerchief, he dabbed at his tears, and added, with a sly smile, "So my dear, were you aware of this? About Rick?"

Lizzie's own sly expression lingered on his for a moment before she said, "I'd say I had a pretty good idea."

Then, after she and Lord Crimson were done exchanging knowing looks, Lizzie said, "You know, Rick, I don't believe I was properly informed about this little cigar-smoking habit of yours."

Rick's reply was a twinkle in his eye, and an expertly crafted smoke ring rising lazily from his lips.

And so, with Lizzie's magic touch, all seriousness ended, and the rest of the evening was spent in light-hearted banter. And had you seen Lord Crimson that night—laughing, joking, making merry—you would never have dreamt, not in a million years, that this was a man who had ever spent an unhappy moment in his life.

But, alas, Rick and Lizzie were needed back in the city, and with only two days remaining, Lizzie found herself being ushered into the room that Alex had, for the last few days, called his own.

"Listen," Alex began. But what he had to say was difficult, and after a moment's hesitation, he tried again.

"Listen—"

"I'm listening, sweetheart. Just spit it out."

"Okay then, here it is—Uncle Charlie's asked me to stay. He's made me his heir, and he wants to groom me in order to run Crimson Industries."

Lizzie's jaw dropped.

"Yeah," Alex said. "Since he doesn't have any kids of his own, and what with the whole Edward Delaney, Susan Sebastian debacle, he's doing what he can to atone for past sins. Actually, he's making me and Francey both his heirs, but he wants me to run the place. He's going to retire and enjoy life for the first time . . . well . . . ever."

Lizzie was devastated. Her little brother, whom she loved more than life itself, separated from her by an entire ocean. It was almost too much to bear.

"Have you decided what you're going to do?" she asked.

"Yeah. I'm going to stay."

Lizzie faltered, but interfering in another's good fortune was not in her nature.

But what of Francey? She'd be heartsick if Alex walked out of her life now. Gently, she mentioned that fact to him.

"I already told her. You want to know what she said?"

Dead silence.

"Okay—she's just completely and totally unbelievable. She said that we were going to have to wait another eight years anyway, but this time there'd only be an ocean separating us, not an endless, centuries-long search. Then she giggled—you know the way she does—and said, 'I think we'll survive.'"

"And what do *you* think?" Lizzie asked.

"You want to know what I think?—Well, when you take into account the reason that I came to New York in the first place—you know—to figure out what I was going to do with the rest of my life?—And you consider all that's happened since then, it's kind of made me stop and wonder whether Dad hasn't somehow figured out a way to stay on top of things."

Alex stood up, pulling Lizzie onto her feet, and took her in his arms. "This is all okay with you, Lizzie, isn't it?"

"Of course, sweetheart," she said, bravely holding back her tears. "Of course it is."

The next night, their final night in England, Rick and Lizzie were lazily walking the perimeter of Uncle Charlie's estate. In silence, they meandered through the English countryside, while a sky blanketed with stars kept careful watch over them. The turmoil, gone from Rick's universe, had been replaced by a simmer, low, but warming steadily. The myriads of stars focused themselves upon that simmering and now it all but boiled over.

"Lizzie?"

She'd been looking up at the sky, lost in thought about so many things. She turned to him.

"Listen," he said. "I've been thinking . . ."

Her hopeful eyes searched his, and she wondered if he could hear her beating heart.

"Okay," he said, continuing to gather his courage. "So, as I was saying, I've been thinking . . ."

An eternity had passed since last he'd held a woman, and Rick was feeling on shaky ground. But fortunately for all concerned, Lizzie's patience had run out. Rick watched her arms wrap 'round his neck; he felt her draw him close. And as their lips met at last, what he'd felt each time she'd touched or held his hand was magnified in too many ways to describe.

No further words were necessary. Rick and Lizzie belonged together; no less than Edward Delaney and Susan Sebastian; nor any less than Alex and Francey. But those last two—they would have to wait a bit longer.

She sat on her bed. Though Uncle Charlie's only words had been that he hoped she'd be comfortable here, Francey could feel a specialness about the room she'd been given. And she set out, determined to discover its secret.

On the walls were several framed photographs. Mostly they were of a girl, perhaps twenty-one or twenty-two years of age; though in a few of the pictures, a young man stood at her side. The photos were old, discolored with age; and a poignant sadness seemed still to linger nearby. Francey went to the desk by the window and sat down. In a corner was a stack of letters; she ran her finger along the edges. They, too, were very old, and to her sensitive touch, had the feel of love letters. When she could bear the mystery no longer she stood up, intending to find Uncle Charlie. She turned to the doorway, and he was there.

"You're curious about this room, aren't you, my angel?"

With wide eyes, Francey nodded.

He took her by the hand, and together they went to the picture she had looked at first.

"That's my Clara," he said, simply.

Francey glanced at a nearby photograph—one with the young man standing by her side.

"Then, that's you?"

"Yes, my treasure. Can you believe I was ever so young?"

"What happened Uncle Charlie? Please tell me. What happened to Clara?"

He led her to a chair in the corner where he bade her sit down. He walked to the large picture window, and as he watched the setting sun, he told the story. He left out nothing—not her pregnancy, nor the stillborn child—not his decision to end his life, nor his final promise to Clara.

"Darling, there's no need for tears," he said, for they were streaming from her eyes. "Not any longer, for the story has a happy ending."

And Francey waited to hear how Clara's story, the tragedy of which was almost beyond comprehension, could possibly have ended happily.

"Today," Uncle Charlie said, "I went to Clara's resting place to let her know that I had kept my promise. And as I knelt before her grave a feeling came over me transcending anything I could ever have imagined. She'd taken me in her arms, you see, to let me know that all was finally well; and with a kiss she said good-bye and left this Earth forever.

That night, while Rick was tucking Francey in, she told him the story of Uncle Charlie and Clara. She held his hand during the telling because she knew it would remind him of her mother. When she had finished, Rick stood up and turned away. Lost, he barely heard his daughter's voice.

"Pop?"

He turned. "Yes, sweetheart?"

"It's been quite an adventure, hasn't it?"

It appeared that Francey had developed a gift for the understatement, for he doubted that an adventure such as theirs happened more than once in a thousand years.

"Listen . . . Francey . . ." He sat down and took his daughter's hand. "You can't remember her, of course, but you might have had a mother . . . once."

Her heart pounding, her fingers trembling, the story Francey had waited her entire life to hear, was, at last, unfolding.

"Her name was Sally." Rick steadied himself. It was the first time, since her death, that he had said her name aloud.

"We met in a museum. The Guggenheim. I guess I've been remiss in your education insofar as art is concerned. But I'll take you there soon. Okay, sweetheart?"

Francey was already too spellbound to move a muscle in reply.

"Anyway," Rick continued, "in case you weren't already aware of it, the Guggenheim is quite a prestigious place, and they were having a showing of contemporary architecture. A rendering of a building I'd designed was part of the exhibit and I went, on opening day, to check it out—you know, make sure it was properly lit—that kind of thing. When I'd located it, there was a girl, maybe a little younger than I was, and just the most beautiful little thing you could ever imagine, standing in front of it. She was so fascinated that she refused to move, frustrating the heck out of a whole crowd of people wanting a turn of their own. So I forced my way through in order to get a better look at this devoted fan of mine, and I guess I was a bit too obvious, because she gave me this . . . well . . . Let's just call it a not-so-pleasant look. But I said 'hi,' anyway, and she just went merrily along, ignoring me. So I regrouped and tried again. This time I asked her what it was she found so fascinating about the structure, and in a desperate attempt to get rid of this guy who she assumed was just some creep, trying to pick her up, she told me, in no uncertain terms, that what she found so magnificent about it was something that I, in my wildest dreams, could never hope to understand."

Rick paused for a moment to dry Francey's tears with his fingers.

"So I said thank you. And she said, 'You're thanking me for making a mockery of your intelligence?' And I said no—I was thanking her for saying there was something magnificent about the building. Well, it took only a split second for her to realize who I actually was, and you should've seen the look on her face. I knew instantly that we would be together forever."

For an hour or more, Rick told Francey little anecdotes and lengthy stories, and when he was done with the telling, the child wept, for she now knew her mother as well as if they'd spent their lives together.

"There's something else," Rick said, "not entirely unrelated, that I'm pretty sure you're going to find interesting."

At this, Francey quieted her sobs.

"No one," Rick said, "could ever replace her—my beautiful Sally—but I've found someone who has actually managed to patch up the hole in my heart that has remained untended ever since she left. She's actually quite a good friend of yours."

Francey's eyes opened wide, and with a joyous scream, she threw her arms around her father. When she was finally able to speak, and laughing and crying at the same time, she said, "Oh Pop—Oh Pop—I'm so happy, I could burst!"

The next morning they all took a last trip to the property on which the new Crimson Manor was to be built. The site, overrun with dozens of construction workers and several huge machines, was already buzzing with activity. Francey and Alex, thanks to Mr. Portico, had arrived earlier and were comfortably settled in the uppermost branches of the oak tree. Rick and Lizzie, holding hands, were having a final conversation with Uncle Charlie.

"This should work out rather well, don't you think?" Uncle Charlie was saying. "My aircraft is at your disposal, so anytime anyone wants to come and visit, my pilot is a mere phone call away."

Uncle Charlie glanced upward—the laughter from atop the oak tree filling him with joy—and said, "An heir at last."

He turned back to Rick and Lizzie, and with a smile that seemed to light up the countryside, he said, "Now remember, you two—when construction is completed, the first grand event held in New Crimson Manor will be the wedding of Rick and Lizzie."

"We can hardly wait," Lizzie said, squeezing Rick's hand.

"Hey guys, it's time," Rick called out.

Like two little monkeys, Francey and Alex scrambled down through the branches. Uncle Charlie took Francey in his arms.

"My darling, my darling—promise me you'll visit often."

Her answer was a squeeze around his neck that almost cut off his air supply.

With tears in every eye, Uncle Charlie and Rick embraced.

"I don't have the words," Uncle Charlie said. "I've tried to conjure them up, but they do not exist."

Rick didn't even attempt a reply.

"Alex?" The voice was Francey's.

He turned to her and said, though she already knew it, "I'll be right here, or anywhere you want me to be, when you're ready."

Uncle Charlie put his arm around Alex's shoulder and gave it an affectionate squeeze. Together they turned, and as they walked off, Uncle Charlie was heard saying, "Come, my boy. I believe you have a few things to learn . . . if you're to run an empire."

They stood watching until Alex and Uncle Charlie had disappeared beyond a nearby hillside; then, with the little girl in the middle, and all three of them holding hands, Rick, Lizzie, and Francey walked toward the Rolls-Royce limousine, where waited Mr. Portico.

Lizzie spoke first. "You know, Rick, it suddenly occurs to me that I don't really know anything about you."

"That's funny," he said. "Now that you mention it, I don't know anything about you, either."

And when Francey had finished giggling, she said, "You're both just silly."

INTRODUCTION TO THE EPILOGUE

PERHAPS, MY GENTLE reader, you have found in your vast and varied literary adventures that sometimes, though the written page has come to an end, you are left, still, with a feeling of . . . curiosity . . . or perhaps desire for just a bit more. If such is not the case here, then tarry no longer with Francey and company and look elsewhere for further adventures. But if this strikes a chord with you, and the discovery of how everything played itself out would be of interest, then read on, and the loose ends will be neatly tied up for you.

EPILOGUE

THE FIRST THING Lizzie did when she got home was to call Uncle Jules. She related everything that had happened, except for one crucial detail. That, she wanted to tell him in person; and so, the following morning, Lizzie, Rick, and Francey jingled their way through Uncle Jules' entranceway to find him already seated at the wonderful table they'd all come to look upon as their own. Hugs and kisses were exchanged, and everyone sat down.

"Uncle Jules," Lizzie said, still preparing her thoughts.

"Yes, darling, you have my curiosity at a fever pitch, so please—"

"All right," she said. "You like Francey, right?"

Uncle Jules gazed lovingly at the little girl. "As God loves his children."

"And you like Rick too, don't you?"

"My dear—I love Rick. And I love Francey. And if God forbid you are planning to ask how I feel about you and Alex—"

Lizzie reached over and took his hands in hers. "Once upon a time—long, long ago—you told me a story which ended in your becoming a minister. Tibetan, wasn't it?"

For a moment, Uncle Jules said nothing. He noted Rick's sly expression, and Francey's blinding smile. Then, with the twinkle in his eye bouncing from the rooftops, he said, "I'll check my calendar. With a little creative juggling, I should be able to make the time for this."

Uncle Jules never lost his sense of humor.

The wedding was an intimate affair. Uncle Jules, of course, was the officiating minister, while Johnny Falstaff was Rick's best man. Francey played the maid of honor and Alex's role was that of the ring bearer. And any attempt to appear serious and somber went by the boards, as Uncle Charlie joyously gave the bride away.

Five years later, Alex, having turned twenty-one, was given governing control of Crimson Industries. He had proved to be a more than apt pupil, diligently learning the business from the ground up in an astonishingly short time, and Uncle Charlie had no qualms at all about relinquishing the helm to his adopted son, thus making Alex the youngest billionaire in history.

Three years after that, Francey turned eighteen, and after a courtship of three hundred forty years, the lovers' stars finally uncrossed, and Francey and Alex were wed at last: an epic fairy tale, traditionally concluded; i.e., they lived happily ever after.

Finally, and some could misread this as ending on a sad note, but if we pay careful attention and stick this through to the very end, that this is not the case at all shall be borne out.

For three years, Francey and Alex had been living in New Crimson Manor, where the entire west wing was theirs to call home. One evening, after dinner, Francey received a phone call. After she'd hung up, and with her face drained of color, she turned to Alex and Uncle Charlie who were immersed in a friendly game of backgammon.

"Guys," she said, her voice, trembling. "That was Lizzie."

Alarmed, Alex quickly went to her and stood close by, should she need the support of his shoulder.

"It's Uncle Jules," she said. "He's dying."

Two hours later, the Boeing Business Jet was airborne, with Francey, Alex, and Uncle Charlie aboard. The throttle was to the floor, and they were heading, full steam, for New York City.

A mention should be made here that over the past several years, Uncle Jules and Uncle Charlie had become the best of friends. Several times a year, thanks to the comfort and convenience of Uncle Charlie's aircraft, Uncle Jules made the trip overseas. Those times they'd spent together, relaxed in front of a roaring fire, brandy and cigars in hand, and swapping the most amazing stories imaginable, would be missed, terribly, by Uncle Charlie.

The plane was met on the runway by a limo sporting diplomatic plates, thus ensuring that the traffic laws of New York City would be of no hindrance to them that day. Just a small favor Uncle Charlie had called in from an unnamed source at the U.N.

Waiting at Uncle Jules' place of residence, Rick and Lizzie let them in; quietly, affectionate greetings were exchanged.

Now his adopted family was gathered around his bed, and one by one, Uncle Jules said good-bye. Finally, and too weak even to lift his arm, the old man motioned with his finger for Francey to come close. Privacy was desired; everyone else withdrew.

Francey sat at Uncle Jules' side and watched her thoughts drift back in time. She smiled, remembering how she had created such a wonderful effect on him when just a tiny little girl. She recalled the installation of the additional bookshelves made necessary because every time she had gone to visit Crimson Manor, Uncle Charlie had somehow got hold of entire sets of the rarest and most amazing books imaginable, with instructions to add them to Uncle Jules' collection. She thought of how, after she and Alex were married and living in England—on every occasion that she crossed the Atlantic to visit Rick and Lizzie, which was sometimes several times a month—every single time, Uncle Jules received a visit from her.

And, finally, she thought of the room in the back—the sacred chambers to which so few people were allowed access, where, over the years, she and Uncle Jules had spent hour upon endless hour poring over the rarest of the rare volumes. Talking, laughing, weeping. She choked back a sob; how lonely it would seem . . . after he'd gone.

As still as death, Uncle Jules lay. His head, propped up with a pillow, and his eyes, gently shut. Francey took his hand and put it to her lips.

"Hello, sweetheart," he said, with barely open eyes. "I'm glad you made it in time."

Her words stuck hard in her throat, and there, even on his deathbed, it remained Uncle Jules' job in life to make those he loved, comfortable.

"My wondrous little girl . . . You know better than anyone else alive that there's no reason to be sad. But I must say, I do find it heartwarming to know that I have the love of the most miraculous child who has ever walked the face of the Earth."

"Oh, Uncle Jules." Francey said, as she burst into tears.

Bringing all his remaining strength to the task, Uncle Jules squeezed her hand, so she quieted her sobs and listened.

"Above all," he said, "you must always and forever keep in mind all that we've been through together—you and I—and know that there is one thing in life that is as certain as death. And that is—we will all be back. A fact, my darling, which goes double for me."

A half hour later, Francey came out of Uncle Jules' bedroom and quietly closed the door behind her. Her eyes were red, and her face was streaked with tears, but the sorrow one normally feels for the passing of a loved one was absent. She was at peace with Uncle Jules' death. For she had been there herself; and their paths would cross again.

With Uncle Jules' passing, Lizzie felt there was no longer anything left holding her in New York. After a very brief discussion with Rick, who'd been wanting to pack up and leave ever since Francey and Alex had been married, and with Johnny Falstaff's sad blessing, she and Rick moved to London.

It took only a few days for Uncle Charlie to push the necessary paperwork through the British bureaucracy, and Rick and Lizzie, just like that, had dual citizenships and a license for Rick to open his own place of business. As a favor to Johnny, Rick structured his company as an extension of Johnny's New York based firm. *Falstaff and St. Michael, Architects*, it was named, and gave Johnny more than ample excuse for him and Kate to make frequent visits to London, ostensibly to ensure that Rick was doing a good job running the overseas branch. Needless to say, he was.

My patient reader, there is yet one last thing essential to this story to relate; some might even find that the reason for this entire narrative is contained in this, the final thought.

One year after moving to London, Rick and Lizzie found themselves in possession of a grandchild. And a few days after he'd made his entrance into this world, that child—one Charles Jules Gingery—awoke from his nap to find his entire loving family surrounding him. Admiring her little boy and basking in the adoring attention he was receiving, Francey noticed something. She looked harder, not quite believing her eyes. Questioningly, she turned to Lizzie who confirmed, with silent astonishment, that she had seen it also. Excitedly they clutched each other, and together they turned once more to the child. It was undeniable. There, bursting forth from little Charlie's gaze, was the same wise expression and unmistakable twinkle they'd seen in Uncle Jules' eyes so many times before.